Back to One: Take 2

Ambient Light

By Antonia Gavrihel

Hidden Shelf Publishing House
P.O. Box 4168, McCall, ID 83638
www.hiddenshelfpublishinghouse.com

Artist: Megan Whitfield

Editor: Robert D. Gaines

Graphic design: Allison Kaukola

Interior layout: Kerstin Stokes

Publisher's Cataloging-in-Publication data

Names: Gavrihel, Antonia, author.
Title: Ambient light / Antonia Gavrihel.
Series: Back to One
Description: McCall, ID: Hidden Shelf Publishing House, 2022.
Identifiers: LCCN:2022909659 | 978-1-955893-11-4 (paperback) |
978-1-955893-12-1 (Kindle) | 978-1-955893-13-8 (ebook)
Subjects: LCSH Motion picture actors and actresses--Fiction. |
Celebrities--Fiction. | Marriage--Fiction. | Women--Fiction. | Famil-
-Fiction. | Man-woman relationships--Fiction. | Romance--
| BISAC FICTION / Family Life / Marriage & Divorce | FIC
Friendship | FICTION / Romance / Contemporary
Classification: LCC PS3607.A87 A63 2022 | DDC 813.6--dc23

Table of Contents

The Journey Continues: *Back to One* 5
1 The Dance 6
2 Two Become One 12
3 A Private World 15
4 Kyle's Career 16
5 Love and Family 24
6 Wish List 29
7 Bambina 33
8 Curtain Call 40
9 Little Feet 44
10 Starstruck 46
11 Better Now 48
12 Valley of the Sun 51
13 Old South 56
14 Fields of Gold 61
15 The Labyrinth 66
16 Piercing Heat 71
17 The Walk 78
18 Uncle Oscar 83
19 Crashing 87
20 Winning and Losing 90
21 Blink of an Eye 94
22 Gathering Storm 104
23 Secret Life 109
24 Howling at the Moon 112
25 Uninvited Guest 117
26 A Ray of Hope 123
27 Suspension of Disbelief 126
28 Hurdles and Locked Doors 131
29 Confessional 133
30 The Star and the Actress 136
31 The Measure of a Man 140
32 Catch Me When I Fall 144
33 Glow of Dawn 147
34 A Stroke of Genius 149
35 Westlight 152
36 There's No Place Like Home 154
37 Heroes and Other Illusions 161
38 Road Less Traveled 166
39 Way Down 170
40 What You Deserve 172
41 Accolades 175
'2 A New Direction 179
⁴3 Sunrise Over the Hollywood Hills 180
44 Our Story 183
Biography 186
Preview: *Cinéma Vérité* 187
Exclusive Bonus: *Way Down* - The Movie 188

To my real-life big brother, who helped raise me into the person I am today by never allowing me to take a shortcut or give up on my dreams. Thank you for your patience and your loving support all my life.

Ambient Light: The natural light that is already present in a film scene—soft, directionless, and free from shadows before any artificial lighting is added.

The Journey Continues . . .

Friendship is a Single Soul Dwelling in Two Bodies.
-Aristotle

*B*ack to One, Antonia Gavrihel's novel preceding *Ambient Light*, is the story of a perfect friendship. Cate and Kyle are two people who never should have met, who become dearest friends amidst society's suspicions about the existence of such love and devotion. In an age of cynicism and rough waters, a platonic relationship is not only rare but nearly mythical.

Kyle Weston is one of the biggest movie stars of his generation. A divorced man with a five-year-old son, Scott, Kyle lives the true Hollywood lifestyle in his posh Malibu beach house.

Cate Leigh is a married, transplanted Californian who lives in Montgomery, Alabama, with her husband, Alex, and their three-year-old son, Robbie.

While visiting her entertainment attorney brother, Edward, in Los Angeles, Cate meets Kyle at a studio party in Beverly Hills. Their connection is immediate and undeniable. In spite of the scrutiny of the press and the ensuing gossip, they dare to develop a strong friendship. It is a relationship based on respect, understanding, likeness, and healthy boundaries. A true and trusted friend had been a missing piece for both. Their alliance not only enhances life but defines it.

Cate's marriage falls apart unexpectedly, her husband leaving her for another woman. Sustained by her bond with Kyle, Cate opens the door to a new life and career back in Los Angeles.

In the face of their denial, Cate and Kyle's attraction continues to grow, a quiet understanding that their friendship is most important ... until the day Kyle risks losing his special bond with Cate to reveal his deep love and passion for her. The first story ends as perhaps only time and circumstance would ever allow ... the two as one.

Back to One: Take 2 Ambient Light begins just hours after the first book ends.

Chapter 1
The Dance

K yle fumbled with the keys, the ambient light from within the house inviting them to enter. As the door opened, Cate drew him to her for another passionate embrace, her body rising to meet his, their lips pressing hungrily. Kyle swept her up in his arms, kicked the door shut, and carried her into the bedroom. He gently set her down on the bed, time and space giving way to desire. At last, they were one.

Kyle knelt before her, staring into the radiance of Cate's deep brown eyes, tracing her lovely face with his touch. The anticipation, the longing, was feverish, her breathing shallow and craving. Kyle kissed her softly, allowing the impulse to rise and overtake them, awakening a deep-rooted yearning. Wantonly present, there was only now.

The flames in the fireplace delicately lit the room, painting shadows and shapes on the ceiling and drenching them in the sheen. Cate pushed herself back towards the head of the bed. Kyle saw the silhouette of her hands shake as she began to unbutton the front of her dress.

He tenderly took her hands in his to stop them from trembling.

"I love you," he whispered.

Cate's rapture shone in her eyes. "I trust you."

The sound of her words echoed through her awareness. They were undeniably true and yet uncommon—a momentary realization that she had never experienced complete love until now. Every touch, every kiss, every look was electrifying. Her body and soul were now a part of this remarkable man.

6

He pulled back to recognize her stunning beauty, and she blushed from his gaze. There were no words, only a flood of powerful feelings of love blending with desire as she lay down, her long silky auburn hair fanning out around her head, reflecting the fire's shimmer. Cate reached her arms out before her, beckoning Kyle to be with her.

It was a sensual revelation to discover the nuances of the other, listening to the soft sighs and quick breaths, the sensation of heat from their bodies, tasting their lips and moans. All senses were alive.

They made love throughout the night, taking only brief respites to revel in the afterglow of gratification.

The morning was breaking, spilling between the blinds, softly alerting Cate and Kyle of their life's new direction. Having eluded sleep, they drifted in and out of the twilight.

Kyle breathed in the scent of her subtle perfume, Cate resting comfortably in his arms. She moved ever so closer, her soft and velvety skin warm against his.

Lost in his embrace, Cate attempted to hold onto the aura of pleasure cascading through her body and mind. She was filled with overwhelming ecstasy.

"That was incredible," she sighed.

"It was perfect." He caressed her face, gazing into her eyes. "It was ..." Kyle shook his head at a loss for words. There was no uneasiness, only deep affection and zeal.

"Like a dance," she reflected.

"We've never danced quite like that," he kidded.

Blushing, Cate lowered her eyes.

"I think that may have been the first time I ever *really* made love." Kyle stared at the smoldering embers in the fireplace.

"I never loved ..." She halted her words and fondly agreed, "Me too."

He drew her close and kissed her earnestly. "I love you. Marry me."

"Wherever, whenever," she said eagerly.

"The sooner, the better," he proclaimed.

"We could find a justice of the peace while we're here," she suggested.

"No, I want our wedding to be a huge celebration … like the one we crashed in New Orleans … even better. I want our guests to be blown away." Kyle adjusted the pillows, making himself comfortable.

Cate nuzzled closer to him. "You sure? It sounds like it might take a while to arrange," she warned.

"No, there are people we can pay to put it together for us." Kyle took another deep breath, still entranced by her perfume. "I want to give you everything. You deserve it."

She turned her sight upwards to him. "You're going to spoil me."

"That's my goal in life," he grinned.

He concentrated, formulating a clever idea, "What if we fly the entire family with us and have our wedding in New Zealand? I've filmed there. It's beautiful. It's getting cold here, and it's early summer in the Southern Hemisphere."

"Kyle, New Zealand would be wonderful." Cate leaned forward. "But isn't that a long flight? It might be a little hard on family members like my mom."

"It's a thirteen-hour direct flight. We'll arrive a couple of days early to rest and get over the jet lag." He stared into her eyes reassuringly. "Promise you'll let me handle everything?"

"Okay, thank you!" Cate sat up excited, catching the covers before they slipped off.

Jumping out of bed, Kyle grabbed his jeans from the floor and pulled them on.

She watched him get dressed. "You know, we could have been together hours sooner if we had stayed in New Mexico instead of chartering a plane to get here."

Kyle sat down on the side of the bed and faced her.

"No, I wanted our first time to be in this room. I built the ranch for you. It's our home." Kyle brushed back her hair. "You know, I've imagined this moment for some time."

"Really? When did that start?" Cate cuddled up to him.

"Aruba."

"Yes, Aruba was special." Cate shyly glimpsed away.

Kyle paused, searching her demure expression, and silently drifted back to the memory of their trip. His gaze made her vulnerable.

"So, it wasn't the moment we met at the party in Beverly Hills?"

Cate joked self-consciously. She inhaled slowly and reminisced, "All those attractive women surrounding you ... and suddenly you appear on the balcony above the gardens ... just the two of us."

"Spring of 2005," Kyle interjected. "Three and a half years ago. Back in the days when I was somewhat of a rascal."

Cate's face reddened. "To be honest, that first night, I tried my best not to be seduced by those blue eyes of yours," she fondly admitted. "You weren't a rascal with me."

"Never. You're my best friend." He revealed, "However, I do remember one extremely sensuous night." A devilish smile crossed his face.

"When was this?" Cate was stunned.

"After Aruba, in New Orleans. I had a rather vivid dream about us making love," Kyle confessed.

"Wait!" She abruptly sat up, wrapping the covers about her, "I remember. The next morning after the wedding, you were acting so odd. You mentioned you had a dream, and you wouldn't tell me."

"I couldn't. It was pretty intense." Kyle's grin spread, recalling the details. "Last night was so much better."

"You're such a romantic."

"With you, I am." He stroked her cheek with the back of his hand.

Cate scanned the room. "You know our bags are outside at the front door. We never brought them in. I guess we were a little preoccupied."

"Wonder if they're still there? Oh, wait! We're in the middle of nowhere," he teased, putting on his shoes.

"Is there something I can wear in the meantime?" Cate glanced down timidly.

"Are you being shy?" He handed her the buttoned-down shirt he had worn the night before. "Here."

Cate modestly slipped on the shirt before sliding out from beneath the covers. When all buttoned up, she struck a pose, her arms out. "Not exactly the alluring negligee I'd envisioned for our first night."

"Very sexy if you ask me," Kyle said.

"Seriously?" She scrunched her face. "I always wore clothes like this around the beach house." Cate inspected the shirt hanging on her from different angles.

"Yes, you did." He ogled at her.

"Kyle Weston, you never said a word!" She crossed her arms.

"What was I supposed to say?" he chuckled. "You look hot? I wasn't allowed those kinds of thoughts, *friend*." Kyle brought her in close and kissed her urgently. "At this rate, we'll get nothing done today, and we have a lot to do."

"We do?"

"Uh-huh. Buy some groceries and make lots of calls. We have to plan a wedding. I should phone Ruth."

"Why?"

"Because that's why I have an assistant. She can help coordinate all of this and put out the press release. And it's important to talk to the whole family before ..."

"Wait," Cate interrupted. "Press release?"

"The instant I make the first call, the tabloids find out. I'd rather control the gossip."

"Can't we enjoy it for even one day?" Snuggling against his chest, Kyle wrapped his arms around her.

"Not a minute to waste." He grabbed his cell phone and gave it to her. "Here. You first. Call your brother and your mom and tell them the news. Oh, and it'll be about a ten-day stay in New Zealand for the wedding. It's close to the holidays, so school's winding down for the boys and Emily, and I'm sure Ed will be able to shuffle some things at the firm. We'll tell the boys in person when we return Sunday. I need to ask Robbie for permission to marry his mom. After all, you belong to him."

Kyle's consideration stirred Cate's very soul.

Cate's brother wasn't surprised, declaring it was about time. Edward vowed to keep it under wraps until they returned Sunday and watch Robbie for them so they could coordinate plans from their Montana hideaway.

Cate's mom was so thrilled she began yelling the news to her sister, Mary before Cate could give her the wedding details.

Cate was amused, handing Kyle back his phone.

"Mom's the town crier, and Aunt Mary's the bellringer. They'll keep the secret for maybe half a day before they blab to everyone. You might need to get a hold of Ruth now."

Kyle removed Cate's phone from the side pocket of her bag and gave it to her. "Then you have about an hour before the word gets out."

Cate turned to grab her toiletries from her bag to take a shower. Kyle caught her hand, examined her eyes, and asked, "Any regrets?"

"Only that we waited this long." Cate kissed him on the cheek.

"We'll make up for lost time." He kissed her hand, spinning his finger in a circle in front of him, "Go. Get ready."

Cate heard him on the phone giving Ruth details and instructions. This was indeed her very own Hollywood fairytale.

Chapter 2
Two Become One

*T*he North Island resort, situated on the top of a hill with breathtaking views of the surf below, was elegant. The rooms were comfortably refined, and the atmosphere was idyllic. The extravagant spectacle was impeccably executed, the resort transformed into a romantic paradise.

Family members arrived with Cate and Kyle a week before the celebration to relax and tour the beauty of New Zealand. A couple of days before the weekend, to Cate's great surprise, Kyle flew in friends and business associates at his expense to match the expectation of an elaborate wedding. With little notice, everyone had circled their calendar for Saturday, December 06, 2008.

The sky was the richest blue Cate had possibly ever seen. With the panorama of the Pacific Ocean as a backdrop, flowers covered the satin runner stretching to the arched structure on the cliff's side. Flowers were everywhere, even draping the chairs for sixty guests. From the standing floral displays to the trendy attire worn by the guests, the crash of color was blinding with vibrance. The music of a classical string quartet harmonized effortlessly with the birds singing and the waves breaking below.

Scott and Robbie were young groomsmen, standing at the edge of the archway in their tuxedos, squirming to get comfortable. Their grandmother and great aunt sat wiping away happy tears. The maid of honor, Emily, resembled a princess in a pastel rose-colored gown. Her father, Edward, relishing the role as Kyle's best man, watched with pride for his sister's cue.

The music melodically flowed into Train's *Marry Me*, superbly orchestrated for Cate to walk down the aisle.

Kyle never looked more like a classic handsome movie star as he waited for Cate under the archway with the expanse to the horizon. Cate saw only Kyle. Everything else faded away. She realized there was no doubt or worry on his face, no hesitation. With every step toward Kyle, she became more relaxed and serene.

The moment Kyle saw Cate almost floating to him, he could no longer catch his breath. She was his beautiful angel dressed in a jaw-dropping white long-sleeve illusion sheath with a plunging V-neck and a corset bodice. There was no veil, simply a tiny diamond tiara-shaped headpiece, enough to give a glitter in her flowing auburn hair. For an instant, he remembered hearing the distant drums in Aruba foretelling this moment ... their long journey's destination. The pieces of the past were revealed in their present, and together they had a new life with a limitless future.

Captured in the flush of unconditional love, Cate and Kyle's voices lifted unfettered on the ocean breeze, pledging their devotion with eager and heartfelt vows sealed with a tender kiss to the rousing applause of their guests.

The reception was over the top—tables full of hors d'oeuvres, three full bars, and a strolling trio of musicians preceding a delicious full-course meal at linen-covered tables with fine place settings and crystal. There was a multi-tiered wedding cake towering on the main table, with a bountiful selection of desserts encircling it. After dinner, a big band and a spacious dance floor launched a new level of celebration—the music, the dancing, the abundance of flowers flavoring the air with competing fragrances. It was a *happening*!

By renting out the entire resort, Kyle hoped the seclusion and extended distance from Hollywood would afford some level of privacy.

However, the onslaught of tabloid reporters to Auckland and the surrounding area caused a need for heightened security to attempt to restrict their access to the function. Unfortunately, it was not effective. The media fascination was beyond insidious.

Seeking solitude, Cate and Kyle honeymooned on a 120-foot yacht anchored in a protective cove off the island of Tahiti. They cruised on their floating resort around the Society Islands, each island with a unique magical quality. To maintain privacy, they would retreat to the magnificent stateroom comprising one whole level of their craft.

Nature also provided entertainment. Each evening, they relaxed in a hot tub on the top deck, drinking champagne and listening to music under an endless canopy of stars. One night, after locating the southern cross within a meteor shower, Cate and Kyle listened to Crosby, Stills, and Nash sing *Southern Cross*, their soundtrack to the heavenly effect.

"Do we live in a movie?" Kyle wondered.

"No," Cate smiled, "it's too perfect."

On the flight back to Los Angeles, Cate and Kyle paged through several tabloid publications that had aerial views of their hilltop wedding. The ceremony, reception, and honeymoon coverage were invasively plentiful, heralding their celebration as easily trumping all Hollywood parties, much less weddings.

Now for the serious business of creating a blissful life together—not only as best friends but as husband and wife in a land where marriages are often doomed ... Hollywood.

Chapter 3
A Private World

*M*olly Lambert was reading the latest issue of her favorite magazine, *Movie Inquiry*, in the kitchen of the D'Amoré Restaurant. The lunch shift hadn't yet begun, so she was alone except for the sous-chef, Bernard.

The magazine featured a story detailing the celebrity wedding of the year. On the cover, Kyle Weston danced with that woman. He was so dashing and handsome in his tuxedo; she was dressed in a slutty white gown with pearl beading on satin and lace. Molly concentrated on every detail of her rival, particularly the massive diamond engagement ring and stylish diamond wedding band.

"Bitch," Molly muttered loudly to herself, not caring if anyone overheard. "She's not good enough for *my* Kyle. She doesn't deserve any of this."

In her opinion, Catherine Leigh wasn't any better than all those other floosies who had tried to compete for Kyle's interest.

"Why her?" she grumbled. "What makes her so different?"

In disgust, Molly took a pen out of her server's pocket, scribbled over Cate's face, and tossed the magazine into her locker.

Before starting her shift, Molly looked at the stainless-steel oven across from her. Her distorted image on the reflective surface was thin and a bit boney. Her shoulder-length blond hair was stringy and in dire need of a root touch-up. Only thirty-five, she looked old and weary. It was as if Molly Lambert had been waiting tables forever.

Chapter 4
Kyle's Career

*T*he cameras flashed as Kyle raised the golden statue, the Academy Award for Best Actor.

After a profound acceptance speech, Kyle waved at the audience and started to exit the stage, giving one final appreciative nod to his lovely wife, who beamed with pride. Cate had predicted this night the year before, exiting the movie theater in their small hometown. Her faith in Kyle was unmatched.

Champagne and congratulations flowed at the Governor's Ball. The place was crowded with Oscar attendees and industry members working the room while partying through the night. One well-wisher after another enthusiastically shook his hand and patted his back. Watching Kyle wrapped in the excitement, Cate stepped back, appreciating how exceptionally hard he had worked to reach this level of success.

As Cate nibbled on the appetizers at the center table, she spotted Kyle cornered by three attractive women. He had a polite but distant expression on his face, no doubt wanting to escape. It reminded Cate of the first time she saw him at the party in Beverly Hills, surrounded by beguiling women, each vying for his attention.

Kyle caught sight of Cate watching him with a look of affection. His face lit up with a bright smile meant only for Cate, the woman he cherished.

Suddenly, someone approached Cate from behind, fondling her arm uninvitingly. Turning, she froze. It was Everett Franklin, one of the executives at the studio. She was first introduced to him at the premiere of *Elk Crossing*. Her gut immediately told her to avoid him, and she'd frequently take refuge behind Kyle whenever Franklin was nearby.

"Catherine, it's been a long time," he announced with an air of smugness. "Congratulations on your husband winning an Oscar."

"Thank you," she said, wishing he'd walk away.

"That was an interesting speech Kyle made ... singling you out. The *love* of his life, huh? Very touching."

"He thanked everyone," she corrected, "including his deceased grandmother."

He glowered at her with a provocative pretense. "Quite an accomplishment for you too, my dear. I mean, landing a powerful, rich celebrity like Kyle as a husband."

Before she could respond to the catty slight, Kyle walked up, reaching his hand toward Franklin. "Hello, Ev, nice to see you."

"I want to congratulate you," Franklin said while shaking Kyle's hand. "I'm not surprised, of course. And I want to thank you again for inviting me to your wedding. Sorry I couldn't attend." He paused and looked directly at Cate. "I hear it was quite an *affair*."

"Thank you." Kyle smiled distractedly, still scoping out the room.

"As always, nice to see you both." Franklin started to leave. He lingered, turning to Cate.

"Catherine, I was thinking we need to schedule a meeting at my office and talk about some of your career choices. I have some ideas, suggestions. See you soon."

"Have a nice evening," Kyle called after him and glimpsed at Cate, who was scowling.

"What is it?"

"*See you soon*," she imitated. "When hell freezes over."

"What?"

"He gives me the creeps." Cate flinched. "You invited him to our wedding?"

"I invited all the studio brass. Ignore it. He's just throwing his weight around. Don't take it personally." Kyle picked up the shrimp from her plate before taking Cate's hand. "Let's see who else is here."

Deciding to hide her discomfort about Franklin, Cate cuddled Kyle's arm. "I know this is a big night for you, honey. You deserve to celebrate, and I don't want to be a party-pooper, but I'm getting tired. And we still have to get to Ed's house."

"Cate, this is business. I have to make connections. How else do you become a success?" Kyle munched on the shrimp.

"Kyle, you just won an Oscar, and you're the highest-paid actor in the business. I think you've made it, sweetheart. Maybe now you can take a breather and spend more time with your sons?"

"And *you*." He kissed the side of her head. "Okay, one more lap around to make sure I've talked to everyone. Then we'll go."

Cate was relieved to arrive at Edward's house, reminiscent of the premiere night of *Elk Crossing*. It had become a family tradition to take the festivities to her brother's home and dissect the events of the evening.

Edward had invited Beverly Quinn, an attractive corporate attorney he had recently begun seeing. She was intelligent and sophisticated, in her early forties, with fashionable brown hair and a kind, considerate nature. However, her real talent lay in a boardroom or negotiation table, where she could be ruthless in her determination.

"After winning the Golden Globe, did you feel confident you'd win tonight, Kyle?" Beverly asked. Edward poured more champagne into everyone's glasses.

"No, not really. I've seen it go both ways." Kyle sipped his champagne.

Edward kicked his feet up on the coffee table. "Tell me, what are you two doing next?"

"I'm shooting in Eastern Europe at the end of summer." Kyle stretched out on the oversized chair. Edward noticed Cate lost in her thoughts, correctly sensing she was dreading Kyle's departure.

"Cate, what will you be doing?" Beverly inquired, sitting on the arm of the sofa next to Edward.

"Tom has a couple of projects for me. One's here in town and the other is a limited series shooting in Denver this fall." She kept her eyes lowered.

"Catherine, you're not going with Kyle?" Edward had a strange guise, scrutinizing his sister.

"I asked her to come with me," said Kyle.

"He's working, and I'll be working too … and there's the boys." She stared at the bubbles in the glass, willing them to carry her away from her feelings.

"Wow, you both are busy," Beverly admired.

"I foresee more awards in your future." Edward held up his glass. "To reaping the rewards of hard work and great talent." Edward glanced at Cate to see her reaction.

"Thank you." Kyle cheered. The three of them drank to the toast. Cate slowly touched the rim of the glass to her lips, barely tasting the champagne. Something about Edward's words struck her as a caution. *Don't forget what makes this worthwhile*, an inner voice spoke. She gazed at Kyle and was filled with loneliness.

Scott slumped on the sofa watching a ballgame with his dad while Cate fixed dinner. Robbie approached his mom and held out a flyer to her. Cate set down the knife she'd been using to chop vegetables, wiping her hands on a kitchen towel, and reached for the paper from Robbie.

"It's my soccer schedule. Next Saturday's the first game."

Cate read the sheet. "Oh, good, Robbie. Your game is first thing in the morning, and Scott's is later in the afternoon. We can make both games easily. We'll even have time for a family lunch in between." She pinned the paper to the front of the refrigerator.

"Make it a light lunch," Scott yelled from the living room.

"Of course, sweetie. Don't want to weigh you down before a game." Cate laughed. "I'll call your mom and John and see if they'd like to join us."

Scott flashed an appreciative grin as Robbie plunked down next to him on the sofa. Kyle rose and made his way to the refrigerator for something to drink.

Sidling up to her husband, Cate asked in a low tone, "You will be there, right, for both games?"

Kyle glanced at the boys, leaping off the sofa when one of the Dodgers belted a homer.

"I doubt I can be at either," Kyle said. "I'm leaving for Dubrovnik in less than two weeks. Since it's my production, I have a lot to coordinate."

Cate leaned in and said in a quiet voice, "Kyle, please, take one day off and be there for the boys. It's so important to them, and you miss so much because of work as it is."

"I don't think I can." Kyle opened the bottle of sparkling water and took a sip.

"Kyle, they're not going to be boys forever." Cate checked to see if the boys were still concentrating on the ballgame. "You're missing your sons' lives. These are the fun days. Let's be a family, okay?"

"You'll be there, right? So, you represent both of us."

"I'm the mom, not the dad. The boys need their father. Please come." Cate tried to maintain a subdued level of speaking. Scott's ears perked up. He strained to listen to their conversation while Robbie continued to be wrapped up in the game.

"I don't want to get their hopes up," Kyle stated. "After this film, we'll have plenty of time together before the next project, okay?" He kissed her, walking back into his study with the bottle of water.

Scott turned to Cate, straddling the sofa. "Thanks, Cate. But what made you think he'd come this time? He never has before."

Robbie's attention was ripped from the game, overhearing Scott's statement.

"What! Kyle's not coming to our games?" Robbie was taken aback, gawking at his brother and mother. Both boys stared at Cate, seeking assurance that she could fix everything.

Cate lowered her head and sighed, helpless to soothe her sons' likely disappointment. She didn't want to promise something she might not be able to deliver. Cate's challenge was to make Kyle understand the family should come first. It pained her that it may rank low among his priorities.

Kyle sat at the outdoor patio, sampling the local cuisine. Dubrovnik was a picturesque city with charm and vitality, but he could only stare into the distance, a somber air about him. Joseph, who had a small but critical role in the production, leaned over the restaurant's wrought iron fence, recognizing his friend's distressed expression.

"I hope you don't look that miserable because the food's bad," his voice declared.

Kyle glimpsed up, dazed. "Huh?"

"So, how's your meal?" Joseph laughed.

"Good." Kyle snapped back to the present. "You wrap for the night? Hungry?"

"No thanks. They fed us on set. I just needed to get out and take a walk."

"Want some coffee?" Kyle grabbed another cup from the set table behind him.

Joseph sat down and poured coffee from the carafe on the table, enjoying the night air. "So? What's bothering you? Shoot not going well?"

"No, the production's fine. Location shooting," Kyle jerked his head. "I miss Cate."

Joseph grinned. "You're supposed to miss your wife."

Kyle had an idea as he tasted his coffee, "You know, you had more to do with Cate and me getting together than you realize."

"No, I do. And Sy does as well. Our brilliant director's plot to get the two of you to watch the kissing scene. He knew you'd put it together."

"You two set me up." Kyle chuckled.

"Everyone knew you belonged together … except you."

"I knew," Kyle peered up assertively.

Joseph blew on his coffee to cool it, cutting his eyes to the side. "Can I ask you a question?"

Kyle poured more coffee into his cup. "Sure."

"I wanted to ask at the wedding, but I knew it wasn't the right time. Anyway, I've been intrigued by your theory and have to know." An impish look crossed his face. "Were you right?"

"Right about what?"

Joseph lowered his voice. "When we talked about how you'd know if Cate would be any good in bed?"

"You're asking about my sex life with my wife?" Kyle squinted his eyes with a half-grin.

"Yeah, I always ask, you know that. Well?"

Kyle's face shined, "Yeah, she's amazing. Better than I dreamed."

"That's great. I wondered because Cate seems so ... innocent."

"Yeah," Kyle joked, "and she uses that really well."

"That's fortunate. It would be terrible to be soulmates and not have chemistry."

Kyle slid his arms forward on the table, holding his coffee and leaned in. "I wouldn't imagine two people could be soulmates without chemistry."

"Yeah, true," Joseph said, bringing the cup to his lips for a drink. "So, what are you doing for your first anniversary? It's coming up in December, right?"

"The sixth. Not sure. Any suggestions?" Kyle sipped his coffee.

"It's going to be hard to top your wedding." Joseph concentrated for a moment, "Hey, you're in Europe. Plenty of romantic places. Rent a chateau for a few weeks."

"Damn, Joseph, great advice!"

"Thanks, maybe one day I'll find someone to woo with my magic. Enjoy, buddy." Joseph raised his coffee cup to toast Kyle.

"I miss you so much," said Cate on her cell phone, looking out of the hotel window at downtown Denver.

"I miss you, too," comforted Kyle from Croatia. "When do you wrap?"

"The end of the week. I'll fly to Montgomery to drop off Robbie at his dad's and then to L.A." She quietly closed Robbie's bedroom door.

"I wrap in a week. Cate, what if, since Robbie's spending three weeks with his dad and Scott's with his mom, you come to Europe? We can meet somewhere fun and have a vacation together for a few weeks. I miss my friend and my wife. Lucky for me, she's the same beautiful woman."

Cate stretched out on the couch in the sitting area. "Kyle, that sounds wonderful, but I don't want to miss Scott's birthday."

"Honey, I've missed a lot of his birthdays due to work. It can't be helped."

"But this time, it can. It's his eleventh birthday, Kyle. That's pretty important. He needs his dad. You don't want him telling his kids someday that their grandfather was too busy to show up, do you?"

"You're right," Kyle said after a moment of reflection. "That's why I love you. You make me a better man."

Cate remained silent, sensing he had more to say.

"I really wanted our first anniversary to be special," Kyle admitted, melancholy in his voice.

Cate slid forward on the couch. "How about, after Scott's birthday, we finally use the prize we won and go back to Aruba for a week."

"Yeah, okay," he said excitedly. "So, Scott's birthday, then Aruba. You're sure you don't want to go somewhere new and exotic?"

Cate rubbed her tired neck, lost in the images of being with Kyle. "Going to the place that changed our lives? That's pretty exotic to me."

After Cate hung up the phone, she picked up her script and checked the call sheet. Grabbing a red pen, she circled the last day of filming.

Chapter 5
Love and Family

cott's face glowed with excitement when Cate and Kyle walked into Julia and John's house for his birthday party. Scott regarded Cate with deep affection, appreciating that his father's presence was her doing.

It touched Cate's heart to see Scott's exuberance when Kyle took a seat near his son to hand him presents from the stack strewn over the coffee table, spilling onto the floor at their feet. The two shared a bonding moment of laughter and joy.

Cate cut cake slices while Julia served them to Scott's friends, watching him vigorously tear open each present. After delivering the last plates to Kyle and John, Julia strolled back into the kitchen, a bright grin adorning her face, and hugged Cate warmly.

"Thank you for bringing Kyle. Look how happy my son is."

"We're family. Family needs to be here for each other, always."

"You know, you're my best friend, Cate. I never thought I'd say that about someone with my ex-husband. Those other women, ugh, were such bimbos. You, my friend, are a miracle." Julia motioned toward Kyle, talking football and finances with her husband. "See, even Kyle's having fun with John."

Crossing to stand beside Julia, Cate licked a bit of frosting from her finger. "We *are* unique."

Julia smiled, looping her arm around Cate's, both gazing at their contented family.

The sliding doors were thrust open. A gust of cool sea breeze whipped Cate's hair about her face. The roar of waves breaking on the shore could be heard merely yards away from the doorway.

"This bungalow is ..." She couldn't find the words.

"I know, this is wonderful," said Kyle. "I love Aruba."

"Me too," she nodded.

"Well, thank you for bringing me, sweetheart. Strange that we won this trip when we were with other people."

"Remember," Cate chuckled, "you told me to share the prize with my husband. Well, I'm taking your advice, husband."

Strolling to the water's edge, they plopped down on the hard, moist sand, leaning against each other.

"Is it weird being back here?" Kyle smashed some sand in his fist, absorbing the sunshine on his skin.

"For me, this was the site I drowned myself in fun, trying not to see what was happening in my own backyard." She nudged him playfully. "And you came here to do what exactly?"

He side-glanced, "Be with you."

"What a strange way to be with me."

"Yeah, it was pretty screwed up."

Readjusting her position on the sand, Cate stared at his charming face.

"What were you thinking, Kyle?"

"What?"

"What do you mean *what*? You brought Tracy. Did you deliberately try to find someone who was the polar opposite of me? I'm sorry, I tried to be nice to her, but ..."

"Catherine Leigh Weston, I've never known you to dislike anyone." He watched with a grin as she pushed herself up.

"I didn't dislike her. I loathed her," Cate bristled. "Especially when Alex informed me that she was his fantasy."

The breeze continued to toss her hair. Kyle brushed it back to gaze deeply into her eyes.

"Cate, I was lost. The whole time I wanted you. I would've traded places with Alex in a heartbeat to have you all to myself. I didn't care about anyone else. But don't think I didn't realize you were busy having fun, and your husband was somewhere else."

25

"I wasn't hiding from my life with Alex," Cate sighed. "It wasn't much of a life. I was trying not to …" She picked up some sand and threw it to the ground.

"What?" He tipped his head to hold her attention.

She squeezed her eyes shut, knowing this would be a big confession. "Admit, Kyle … admit I wanted you … desperately. It was getting harder and harder to fight the feeling. Everything changed here."

With a bit of a laugh, he stroked her head. "Fortunately, we don't have to hide from each other ever again."

"I still get scared," she said, reclining against him, the surf's white foam rolling in to cover their bare feet.

"Why?"

"One day, I'll wake up, and this was only a beautiful dream. Not real. Or something will happen, and it will be taken from me." She hung her head low.

"This isn't a dream." He lifted her chin to examine her hypnotic eyes. "There's nothing more real."

Laying her down in the sand, they kissed passionately. All they could hear beneath the stirring of the surf was their breathing.

Suddenly, Cate broke away, glimpsing around the beach.

"Kyle, we're probably not alone out here."

"Yep," he groaned, helping her up to go inside the bungalow.

On their anniversary night, walking back to their room after a delectable dinner at the resort's restaurant, Cate hugged Kyle's arm.

"I have a surprise for you," she said. "Since we can't fulfill your fantasy of making love on the beach, I have the next best thing."

A flowing cabana tent was pitched in the sand near the water outside the bungalow. The inside of the tent was dreamily lit by candlelight, with a large bed and a small table set up with fragrant tropical flowers and champagne. The tent's ceiling was made from a filmy material to peer out at the stars in the night sky.

"See, I can be romantic too," Cate said.

Kyle motioned toward the bed. "What's that?"

There was a rope of fresh flowers shaped in a circle in the center of

26

the bed. Cate and Kyle stared at each other, instantly recognizing the significance of the roped flowers.

"It's nothing I requested," said Cate.

Both were surprised. They had an identical flower rope lying on the bookshelf at the ranch ... and knew who sent the message.

Propped against the front of the floral rope was a small card. They sat on the bed, Kyle lifting the card. There was an address and note: *Please come for tea tomorrow at 4 pm.*

Cate determined that MeeMac, the Shaman from the bonfire long ago, spoke a derivative of French similar to Cajun or Creole French. "Merci." Cate accepted the tea being passed to her.

MeeMac's grandson Jacob, the young man who had talked to Kyle that night, was interpreting for them.

"MeeMac said you waited long enough."

"For what?" Kyle asked.

"To get married. She told you nearly three years ago who you were."

"I think we had to figure it out ourselves," Kyle said.

MeeMac focused on Cate, sitting next to her. Rattling off words in her foreign language so fast neither Cate nor Kyle could keep up, she reached over to Kyle and put his hand together with Cate's. Jacob began to unravel his grandmother's words.

"She sees you having some rough times. Not with each other, with the world. There will always be someone ready to take pleasure in your pain. So, arm yourself, keeping close to everything and everyone you hold dear. When you feel most hopeless, find solace in the other. Eternally, you belong together, and no one can divide you. You are forever one."

MeeMac kissed Cate and Kyle on the cheek and then placed her hand on Cate's stomach and smiled.

"Blessings and protection to you both."

The visit was over.

Jacob walked them out to the street to locate a taxi. The area was impoverished. Kyle offered Jacob some money.

"No, thank you," said Jacob, waving away Kyle's open wallet. "You can repay us by remembering you're special. And you must care for the other, no matter what."

"We will," Cate vowed.

"Yes, we will," Kyle agreed, putting his arm around Cate and pulling her to him.

Jacob grinned, shut the taxi door, and walked back toward his house.

Riding to the resort, Cate snuggled in Kyle's arms, thinking about the bonfire three years before when MeeMac offered the revelation that they were destined to be one. Still, it came with a warning. In all her joy at finally being with Kyle, perhaps she had forgotten that she was now in the spotlight … a cruel and dangerous world of scrutiny. She clutched Kyle.

He reacted to her earnest hold, "Something wrong?"

Cate cloaked her concerns, not wanting to expose her frailty.

"This was the best anniversary," she uttered.

It was an intimate, relaxing anniversary. Kyle wondered aloud whether they were celebrating their first anniversary or their fifth. For him, their life together began the first moment they met, and no number of days could ever satisfy his need to be with her.

As 2009 ended, Cate was relieved that neither one had a project demanding they be apart, at least for now. They could go home and be a family. It was ordinary, reassuring, ideal …

Chapter 6
Wish List

oaded down with scripts and work from the office, Kyle entered the kitchen through the garage door of the beach house. He maneuvered the door shut, turning around to be confronted by his ex-wife. She stood matronly, arms crossed, rather angry.

Kyle was startled. "Julia, what are you doing here?"

"You do recall we're leaving tomorrow to visit John's folks in Dallas?"

"Yes, I do." He cautiously set down his paperwork on the kitchen island.

"I was dropping Scott off when Cate fainted. I drove her straight to my doctor's office."

"Is she okay? Where is she?" Kyle rushed toward the bedroom, Julia stepping in his path.

"She will be," she said sternly. "She's laying down … you better be good to her, Kyle Weston, you hear me?"

"I'm always good to Cate." He backed away, a little unsettled. "Julia, we're not married anymore. I don't think you can talk to me that way."

"Oh, I have a right to look out for my friend." Julia picked up her purse. "I need to go. I ordered a pizza, the boys are playing video games in Scott's room, and I'll be home in a week. Tell Cate I'll call her tomorrow when we land to check on her. Now you be here for her. Take good care of her." She started to leave and inspected Kyle's stack of work. "And clean up this mess. I tidied up the kitchen a few minutes ago."

Kyle was perplexed. This was a new experience, he thought. Julia had never scolded him during their marriage.

Cate was on the bed with a damp washcloth across her forehead when he entered their bedroom.

"Hi," she smiled.

"Are you all right?" Kyle asked anxiously.

"I'm fine. A little tired."

"Julia just read me the riot act, saying I had better take care of you. What's going on?" He took a seat beside her.

"She's sweet."

"More like frightening. So, what happened?"

"I was a little dizzy, and Julia insisted I go to the doctor," Cate said quietly. "I'm fine. Quite healthy. Nothing's wrong."

"Nothing unusual?" Kyle lifted the washcloth and waved it in the air to cool it off.

Cate exhaled sadly, her misgivings betraying her as she stared off in the distance. "I'm thirty-eight years old."

"Okay, I'm forty-four. So what? How's that relevant?" He placed the washcloth back on her forehead.

"It's not, it's … do you remember when you first brought me to the ranch after the divorce and asked me what I wanted in life, and I mentioned a list, my wish list?"

"I guess." He knitted his brows, trying to recall the memory.

"It had things I desired," she persisted. "A warm home, a happy and well-adjusted son, adventurous travel. And a man who'd love and adore me and be there for me. Does this ring a bell?" Cate gazed lovingly at him.

"Yes, sort of." Kyle looked toward the ceiling, straining to understand.

"Do you recall if there was anything else on my list?" Her guise was broad with charm.

"I do know what wasn't on it. Me," Kyle jested, feeling her cheeks to check for a fever.

"True," she said, affection pouring from her words. "Only because I couldn't say what I wanted most of all was you."

"Well, I'm all yours." Kyle's smile broadened, and he bent down to kiss Cate, then abruptly stopped. "Yes, there was something else on your list. You're not referring to a dog, are you?"

Cate raised herself up a bit, removing the washcloth.

"We'll get a dog soon. But no, not a dog." She squinted with a laugh.

Kyle took a moment to catch his breath, staring into her eyes.

"Cate, are we having a baby?"

She nodded. "Are you happy?"

"Yes! Very!" His eyes glistened with excitement. "A baby!"

"It's so unexpected ..."

"It's wonderful! I couldn't be happier. It's on my list too." He tenderly caressed her cheek as she pushed herself up to sit straighter.

"Kyle, honey, we're not too old to start all over again, are we?"

"Well, you're certainly not," he chuckled.

Cate exhaled with relief.

"We need to tell the boys." She declared, sliding forward to get up.

"They don't know?" He helped her up from the bed and held her arm, walking to the door.

"No, I thought you should know first, and we should tell them together."

Kyle halted. "Hey, how come Julia knew before me?"

"I'm sorry." Cate straightened her dress. "She was in the exam room when the doctor told me."

"Okay," Kyle teased, "you're forgiven."

"I told the doctor we'd celebrated our first anniversary," Cate blushed, "and he said it must have been quite a celebration."

"I do love Aruba," Kyle said with a grin. "Let's have a family meeting."

The gate buzzer rang on Kyle's phone. "We'll be right there," he responded to the alert and turned to Cate. "Pizza's here. Great timing."

Cate jerked to a stop, holding her stomach. "Oh, pizza ... that sounds awful," she moaned. "You three eat alone, and then we'll tell the boys."

"Hey, Scott?" Kyle yelled out the door.

"Yeah, Dad?" Scott called from his room.

"Pizza's at the gate. Would you get it, please?"

"Sure."

Kyle held Cate's arms. She was becoming weaker standing there.

"Oh, no, not again," she groaned.

"What?"

"I had my morning sickness when I was pregnant with Robbie at night. So, I guess it will be the same with this baby too. Night sickness.

Sorry, I feel woozy."

"Can I get you anything?" He tightened his grip on her arms, her legs becoming shaky.

Cate slowly turned her head from side to side, discomfort shown on her face.

"This is new to me. Julia never had morning sickness."

"Lucky lady." Cate was wobblier, "Will you get the boys fed, please? I need to lay down again." She crawled onto the bed and laid still, putting the washcloth back over her forehead and taking deep breaths through her mouth.

"Sorry," he said helplessly.

The corners of Cate's mouth turned up. "You don't have to be. I wish the room would stop spinning, though." She counted on her fingers. "It's for possibly six weeks."

Alarmed, her eyes widened, and she pinched her nose. "The pizza! Oh, no, I can smell it!"

Kyle sniffed the air. "I can't smell a thing."

"Heightened senses. Please eat out on the deck and shut the doors." She began to breathe rapidly through her mouth to ease her nausea.

"Okay, I'll bring the boys in after dinner." Apprehensive, Kyle turned to leave the room and peeked back at her. "You're sure I can't get you anything?"

"Yes, ginger ale, please."

"We don't have any ginger ale," Kyle commented, Cate immediately displaying a forlorn puppy dog gape. "I'll go out and get some," he promised.

Cate smiled weakly. "Thank you. I love you, Kyle."

"Love you, too. Rest."

The door closed, and Cate sought to get comfortable on the bed, keeping the bathroom entrance within her vision.

32

Chapter 7
Bambina

onths went by, making 2010 a busy year as the family prepared for the new arrival. Cate persuaded Kyle to only take projects close to home to spend more time with the family and ensure he'd be in town for the birth.

As Kyle got ready for bed, Cate rested on top of the covers, inspecting the ultrasound picture of their baby.

"You're going to wear out that photo," he laughed.

"We're having a little girl, Kyle," she said with wonder. "A complete family."

"Glad I could help." He winked, laying down low on the bed to be even with Cate's stomach. He lifted her lacy nightshirt to uncover her baby bump and gently placed his hand on it. The baby shifted position at his touch as if reaching for his warmth.

"Wow, that's mind-blowing. Does it hurt?" He glanced up at her.

"No, not at all," she tenderly replied.

"Hey, baby girl," he spoke softly to Cate's belly, "it's your daddy."

"We need to think of a name," Cate suggested. "We can't keep calling her baby girl."

"Want to name her after your mom?"

"Doris? Oh, no," Cate cautioned with a giggle. "My mother would be furious. She's always hated her name. We could name her after your mom and Nana. Elizabeth's a beautiful name."

"I like it better for a middle name," Kyle noted.

Cate studied him silently while he rubbed her stomach, riveted by the baby's shifting position.

"This fascinates you," she said with awe. "Didn't you experience this with Julia and Scott?"

"Not really. I was out of town most of the time. I had to work. I told you I missed Scott's birth. I was on a plane trying to get home."

"Poor Julia, all by herself." Cate touched his face. "No wonder she scolded you, telling you to take care of me."

He smirked, shaking his head. "Well, she had her mom."

"Not the same. I'm so glad you're here. And see, you're still able to work."

"The advantage of having my own production company now." Kyle took a long pause. "So, Alex was there for you?"

"No, not really. I mean, he was home, but …"

"What?" Kyle rolled onto his stomach, propped up on his arms, watching Cate.

"You have to understand, there's a ton of hormones coursing through you when you're pregnant, which makes you … crave affection." She attempted to sound very clinical.

"You mean, it makes you horny?" He chuckled, bobbing his eyebrows. "More than usual?"

"Stop," she joked with a naughty smile, her complexion flushing. "Well, he worked late and ignored me most nights. Might as well have been alone."

"How did you get to be so incredible with a cold man like Alex in your life?"

She sported a cheeky grin. "An active imagination fueled by frustration. And then there's you. You're amazingly skillful." She bent down and kissed him. "Just following your lead."

"So, how are those hormones tonight?" Kyle reached over to switch off the bedside lamp. The moon's glow through the transom light above the shuttered window softly filled the room.

"Raging," she whispered seductively.

Kyle gently kissed Cate's stomach and whispered, "Go to sleep now, baby girl. Daddy needs to make Mommy happy."

34

The boys had become overly protective of their mother in her advanced stage of pregnancy. The only way Robbie and Scott let Cate walk on the beach was for one of them to accompany her. Cate considered it doting and completely unnecessary. Just as she had with Robbie, Cate kept in good shape throughout the pregnancy, exercising and eating healthy, gaining only about twenty pounds, textbook perfect. From behind, you'd never know she was pregnant. Her baby bump was the only giveaway of the forthcoming arrival.

Returning from their stroll, they spoke with Mark Tylare, hanging out on his deck. Mark got into a lively discussion with the boys about school, Robbie now in fourth grade and Scott beginning junior high.

Cate shared her news of an offer she had received to do musical theater after the baby was born, an Equity West Coast production of *Mamma Mia!* with Cate co-starring in the role of *Tanya*. Ronnie Allridge, who had been one of the producers of *Sunset Rise*, was directing the production and insisted Cate was perfect for the comedic role. "Just think," he had said brightly, "all the dancing will get you back in shape after the baby is born!" Cate's only hesitancy was that singing publicly was a recently conquered fear.

The boys were sincerely excited about the play. Unexpectedly, Scott pulled Robbie back a few steps to whisper in his ear.

Grinning, Scott sprinted forward. "Cate, what does *Mia* mean?"

"It's Italian for *my*. Why?"

Robbie caught up and gleefully spouted, "Mom, why don't you name the baby Mia?"

"Yeah, Cate, it's a pretty name … Mia," Scott nodded.

"You know what?" Cate pondered the suggestion. "I love it. And I bet your dad will too. I think you two should mention it to him." Cate put her arms over her boys' shoulders on either side of her. "Certainly, a fruitful walk."

They climbed the stairs to the deck and opened the double glass doors to enter the living room. Suddenly, Cate spasmed and bent forward, letting out a muffled cry of pain. The boys reacted with panic, gripping her arms to hold her up.

When she could speak, she looked up at their frightened faces and measuredly confessed, "My water broke. We have to go. I can't drive.

We'll need to get a taxi to the hospital." Cate made her way into her bedroom.

Scott had a better plan and tore out the front door, flying down the drive.

After a few minutes, Cate came out of the bedroom. She had changed her clothes and had cleaned up. Carrying her overnight bag, her nine-year-old clutched her arm and helped her to the door.

Scott burst through the door. He took Cate's other arm, the three of them exiting the house. Mark Tylare rolled up in his car and ran over to open the passenger car door.

"Oh, Mark, thank you so much."

"Your son's very persuasive," he smiled.

Cate gave Scott a quick cuddle. Mark helped Cate into the seat and jogged back to the driver's side while the boys piled into the backseat. The car took off and sped down the road to the hospital.

Mark reluctantly left them in the nurse's care, who wheeled Cate back to the private birthing suite.

The nurse hooked Cate up to the baby monitor while the doctor examined her. As the medical staff stepped out, Cate called the boys into the room to sit with her.

Cate looked around the room while narrowing her eyes. "Did anyone remember to call your father?"

The wait felt drawn out with each contraction. In reality, it was happening faster than her labor with Robbie, which had been a mere six hours.

Kyle rushed in, frazzled from fighting his way through traffic, trying to regain some sense of balance. He kissed Cate and the boys.

"The boys have been wonderful company," Cate said proudly. "Scott was amazing. He recruited Mark Tylare to drive us here. And Robbie helped me get cleaned up."

"That's great, boys. Thank you." Kyle patted Scott on the back and squeezed Robbie's arm affectionately in acknowledgment.

The doctor came back in and checked the read-out on the monitor.

"You ready, Mrs. Weston? I need to examine you, but I think we're about there."

"Yes, doctor." Cate stretched her hand out to Kyle. "Why don't you go with the boys and have some dinner?"

"Why? I'm not leaving." Kyle held her hand tightly.

"I kind of had a bad experience before. It's unnecessary to be here for this part. Let's not argue."

"What do you mean?" Kyle was baffled.

"Seriously, I love you for wanting to be here. Except this is something I need to do on my own. I guarantee you'll be the first non-medical person to see her once she's arrived."

"But ..."

"No, there's the door. I'm kind of busy here." An even more powerful contraction hit.

"Okay." He kissed her and slowly turned to leave, dumbfounded and anxious.

As the contraction eased, Cate caught control of her breath.

"Honey, you were here for the most important part," she winked.

It had been two hours. Edward and Emily had arrived and sat huddled with the boys discussing something weighty, Kyle stared at the ceiling, feeling useless.

Finally, the nurse summoned, wrenching him from his stupor. Kyle sprung up and hurried to the room, the rest of the family following close behind. Cate had freshened up, radiant, with the baby in her arms, bathed and wrapped in a pink blanket.

"Hi, Daddy. Want to meet your daughter?"

She had silky auburn hair, a healthy six and a half pounds, and had beat Robbie's record by an hour.

"Beautiful," Kyle heard himself say.

The kids and Edward peeked their heads in, and Cate invited them to meet the baby. The little one was alert and frequently turned her head to follow a friendly voice that she heard.

Emily bubbled and cooed at the baby, thrilled to have a girl cousin. "She's so tiny and sweet. What are you naming her?"

"We still haven't decided," Kyle said, holding the precious cherub in his arms.

Cate gestured to Scott and Robbie, urging them to speak.

"Dad, Robbie and I were thinking," Scott began.

"And Mom agrees," Robbie quickly added.

"We should name her Mia," Scott eagerly announced. "What do you think?"

Cate's smile broadened, waiting for Kyle's reaction.

The new father gazed at the three of them. "Mia Weston."

"Mia Elizabeth Weston," Cate corrected.

"Yes, it's perfect." Kyle brought little Mia up to his lips to kiss her on the cheek.

"And Dad and Cate," Scott continued, "Robbie and I talked it over. Mia needs to have good role models."

"Yeah, and it kind of starts with words," Robbie stated. "She's gonna say things we say."

"We think it'll be better if I could call you Mom," Scott told Cate. "I mean, not in front of my mom, but everywhere else. I want to do that."

"And I could call you Dad," Robbie volunteered, looking to Kyle. Everyone in the room took in the proposal with a sense of purpose and delight.

"Calling me *Mom* would make me so happy. Thank you." Cate kissed Scott and Robbie.

"I feel the same way." Kyle hugged them.

As Emily stroked Mia's tiny hand, Edward glanced at his wristwatch.

"Emily, you can fuss over the baby more tomorrow. It's late. We need to let my sister get some rest. Hey, boys, how about staying with us tonight? I suspect, Kyle, that you plan to stay here?"

"Yeah, there's no way you're sending me away tonight." Kyle planted himself in the oversized chair next to Cate's bed. "I'm not going anywhere."

"Thank you all," Cate said warmly. "Ed, Emily, boys … I love you."

"We love you too, Mom," Scott grinned. "Wow, I just called you Mom for the first time."

In the early morning hours, Kyle lazily woke up in the chair. He glimpsed at a sleeping Cate holding the baby on her chest, lulled to sleep listening to her mother's heartbeat. How angelic they both looked. He snapped a photo, a memory to cherish forever. Carefully, he laid down next to his wife, slipping his arm under her neck to hold her close and gently putting his other hand on Mia's back. He could gaze at the two of them forever, he believed.

Chapter 8
Curtain Call

"Roses for Ms. Leigh." The stage manager brought in yet another arrangement for Cate. After months of rehearsal, the musical had opened to rave reviews. Cate was singled out as a breakout talent, and the house was sold out for weeks.

Midway through the run, the lead—Broadway star Gail Proder—came down with laryngitis. Ronnie Allridge cornered Cate at the stage door when she arrived, informing her that she would perform the lead tonight and possibly longer … at least until Gail recovered.

"That's major singing, Ronnie," Cate gasped.

"Cate, you understudied the role."

On the verge of tears, Cate retreated to the sanctuary of her dressing room. Her fear of singing in public was rearing its ugly head … again. *The lead?!* At least, *my family won't be here,* she surmised.

Doris opened the dressing room door.

"Honey, I heard the news. You're playing *Donna* tonight. I can't wait."

"No, I don't want anyone to see this disaster." Cate wiped away her tears.

Doris sat next to her daughter, trying to calm away the stress by squeezing her hand. "Catherine, you'll be brilliant."

Cate put her head on her mom's shoulder like a small child, realizing the endearing bond between them being strengthened by the musical.

"Darling," Doris began, "you once said you needed a mother to tell you all the things you did right in your life. So, I am. You're very talented and so brave. Willing to dare the world to try to stop you. And you're a great mother with a wonderful soulmate in Kyle." She smoothed Cate's hair with her hand, making sure every strand was where it should be. "So, listen to your mother. Go out there and do your best. I believe in you."

Doris took out a tissue from her purse to dab her daughter's tears, Cate moved by her mother's love and pride.

She *could* do it ... her mother said so.

Hitting the final high note clearly on *Winner Takes All*, Cate was ecstatic. The show ended with a standing ovation, her family cheering in the front row.

Doris rushed into Cate's dressing room and threw her arms around her. "Outstanding! I knew you could do it!"

Cate picked up her wrap and purse, amused. "Mom, you told the entire family. What if I had bombed? And who's watching Mia?"

"Don't worry. Emily's taking care of the baby." Doris embraced Cate again. "This was a performance not to be missed. My shining star! I love you, darling."

Doris went out to greet the family, passing Kyle, who ran in and scooped Cate up in his arms.

"Honey, you were incredible! I'm so proud of you. I know that scared the living daylights out of you."

"Terrified," she giggled.

"You conquered it. What a performance!" Kyle was overjoyed for his best friend.

It was drizzly and dreary the night Catherine Leigh played the role of *Donna*.

Molly Lambert sat in the balcony watching the audience more than the musical. For weeks, she had saved up her money to get a ticket. The stage lights spilled out into the first few rows of floor seats, allowing Molly to make out faces from where she sat. It was pure luck that Kyle Weston was seated in the first row. Molly had only come to see her perform, to see what was so special about this woman.

Molly strained to see Kyle's reaction when Leigh took the stage. Even sitting far away, Molly was disturbed to see that Kyle was thrilled with Leigh's performance. Then again, perhaps his presence was a sign of destiny. Yes, Kyle and Molly were fated to be together.

Outside in the mist, the crowd poured out of the doors, making it impossible for Molly to identify anyone, much less Kyle. Craning her neck and rising on her tiptoes, she jostled back through the departing audience as they dashed to their cars to avoid the weather, making her way to the front double-door entrance. Her search was maddening. Where was Kyle? Despair overshadowing her, she turned to leave, giving one last hopeful glance around the area.

Wait, there he was, standing beneath the marquee toward the backstage exit with a group of friends.

Molly moved closer, pretending to read a large poster of the musical, while she wallowed in the euphoria of being only six or seven feet from her true love.

"Thank you all for coming to the show," the shrew said to her friends.

"Wouldn't have missed it for the world, Sis." The man hugged her.

"It was wonderful, Cate," a woman hanging onto the man said.

Molly observed the man, woman, and an older lady leave. Only the adolescent boys stood near Kyle and Leigh.

"I need to drop Scott off at his mom's," Kyle said.

"Thanks for coming tonight, sweetie." Leigh hugged Scott, the older, taller boy, and then addressed the younger one. "Robbie, want to ride home with me?"

"Sure, Mom."

"Where are you parked, honey?" Kyle asked, very gentleman-like.

Pointing directly across the road, Kyle walked her and the one called Robbie to the car while the older one—Scott was it—waited on the sidewalk. Robbie and his mother climbed into the car, rolling down her window to say goodbye to Kyle.

"I'll see you at home, Catie." Kyle kissed her and began to jog back across the road. "You were amazing! I love you."

"I love you, too," the bitch called back.

The words and kiss crushed Molly. Her mind flew. Maybe if Kyle just saw her, he'd remember how much he loved her.

Kyle strode swiftly with Scott down the sidewalk to their car. They were coming directly toward her. Walking with her head down, Molly deliberately bumped into Kyle.

"Excuse me, ma'am." Kyle offered an apologetic nod.

Molly stared directly at him, yearning to capture his attention. But Kyle barely looked at her. He didn't show any signs of recognition. He just kept walking … away. The rejection ripped at her heart.

She tried to lessen the pain. It's not Kyle's fault, Molly told herself. It's dark and rainy, and that boy was distracting him.

Molly glared at the road in the direction Leigh's car had driven. If only Kyle knew, he would surely be her man. But, that woman … she wasn't all that special.

Chapter 9
Little Feet

ate shaded her eyes with her hand across her forehead. It was a sunny spring day in 2012 at the ranch. She surveyed the immediate backyard down to the lake. Kyle sat at the table—a fire pit built in the center—finishing his breakfast with the boys and Mia.

"You know what this place needs?" Cate solicited, watching the ducks land on the water.

"Other than horses for our state-of-the-art stables," Kyle laughed, "which have sat empty for three years?"

"Yeah, Mom, when are we getting horses?" Robbie pleaded.

"Honey, it's more involved than buying one at a pet store. First, we have to hire someone to help us purchase and train the horses. Right, Kyle?"

Kyle glimpsed up for a tick at hearing his name. "Soon, guys. We've both been a little busy."

Scott was helping Mia, sitting in her highchair playing with breakfast. "Okay, Mom, if it's not horses, what does the ranch need?"

Cate turned with a huge smile and silently peered at her whole family until the boys caught her gaze.

"A new family member."

The boys shot accusing stares at Kyle, and, in turn, Kyle's eyes darted up with shock at his wife.

Cate enjoyed the moment and began to laugh.

"A dog, silly."

That afternoon, they drove to the local shelter and checked out the different caged areas, where surrendered pets and abandoned strays waited for forever homes. Feeding time had ended, so many of the dogs had stretched out for an after-lunch nap.

The Weston family viewed several kennels, numerous dogs crowded together, some recovering from lack of nourishment and care. The shelter workers were trying to deal with the animals' needs and restore their health. It was heartbreaking.

A set of eyes summoned the family over to a cage full of sleeping puppies. There was something unique about this pup. He was a golden retriever mix with an entreating, eager expression, climbing over his sleeping companions to get to the gate. Mia was fascinated. As she gently patted the puppy, he turned and licked her hand, tail timidly wagging.

Oakley had found his new family.

Chapter 10
Starstruck

After an abbreviated audition, Cate decided she'd swing by Kyle's production office and persuade him to take her to an early lunch. Kyle's assistant, Ruth, and a rather burly fellow Cate did not recognize were in the glassed-in conference room when she entered. Their conversation with Kyle seemed to be heated. Through the glass, she picked up varied words, particularly danger and security.

Ruth glanced out the window, catching sight of Cate. Hastily interrupting Kyle, she brought Cate's presence to everyone's attention. Kyle muttered something to Ruth, who came out of the conference door, shutting it behind her.

"Cate, how nice to see you," Ruth said graciously. "We weren't expecting you today."

"I can come back if you're busy."

"No, Kyle will be out any minute. May I get you something to drink … coffee, water?"

Cate shook her head, focusing on Kyle closing a thick folder. He walked out of the conference room.

"Hi honey, what a pleasant surprise," he said, giving her a welcoming kiss. "How was the audition?"

"Fast. I wanted to see if you'd like to take me to lunch?"

"Yes, it'd be a privilege," he smiled. "Ruth, we'll be back in a little while. If he comes in, text me, please." Kyle gave Ruth the laden folder.

Cate took the pulse of the room. The tension was palpable.

"Of course, Kyle," Ruth said, clutching the folder tightly in her arms.

The restaurant was teeming with brazen tourists, and several crowded around them requesting autographs. There was a claustrophobic sensation when caged by a mob of fans, and Cate and Kyle tried to make the best of it.

"I'm guessing this was a bad idea?" Cate whined when the last of the autograph seekers left.

"No, it's fine." Kyle surveyed the perimeter of the restaurant as if looking for someone.

Cate analyzed his intensity. "Something wrong?"

"No, getting situated for the location. More coordinating than I expected. Phoenix is a big city." He laid the napkin in his lap, avoiding eye contact.

"Ruth seems to have a lot on her plate. Have you thought about getting her an assistant? Or is that who that guy was?"

Kyle evaded the question, casually passing the breadbasket.

"Cate, you're getting help with your fan communications. Everything okay?"

Elbows on the table, hands folded in front of her, Cate sat forward. "I have first-rate fans." Cate couldn't contain her curiosity any longer. "Honey, what was in that folder you gave to Ruth?"

"Have you received any interesting fan letters?"

She looked sideways at his diversion of her question.

"I received a marriage proposal," she droned. "I think he's thirteen. It's sweet. His mom brought him to *Mamma Mia!* and he's a big fan of *Sunset Rise.* I think I'm his first crush. You know, puppy love." Cate dallied. "Don't worry, Kyle, you're the only man for me."

"I learn the cutest things about you," Kyle laughed and tweaked her nose.

The rest of lunch was uneventful, discussing Kyle's shoot in Phoenix and Cate's in Chicago. Their careers were complicating the life they shared.

Chapter 11
Better Now

ilming in Chicago, where she had often visited extended family growing up, had been more fun than anticipated. So many fond tales and dietary treats.

She missed Kyle in Phoenix and the kids back home. Doris insisted she watch Robbie and Mia at the beach house, and Scott was with Julia. Although Cate and Kyle intended on splitting their parental duties while each was on location, it would only be for about ten days that both parents would be gone.

Better Now was a fresh romantic comedy starring her old friend Benjamin Parker. It was such a carefree script. Her supporting character was funny, street-smart, and infinitely intuitive. Mark Tylare was directing, and most of her scenes were with Ben.

The last time Cate had seen Ben, she told him she was looking forward to developing their friendship to perhaps something more. The next thing Ben knew, Cate was marrying Kyle. That was almost five years ago.

Cate wondered if acting with Ben would be awkward. Her qualms were alleviated when she discovered it was Ben who recommended her for the role. They had great chemistry, and her comic timing was unparalleled.

Ben's career and personal life had progressed in splendid ways. In a whirlwind romance, he married Teresa. They soon had a son, nearly four years old, eighteen months older than Mia.

It didn't take long before they shared photos of the kids and their families.

"My goodness, Cate," Ben said. "Mia's the image of you."

"True, but her personality's all Kyle. She's bold, self-assured, such a flirt. I was a shy child."

"You have a beautiful family," Ben stated after thoroughly scrolling through the photos.

Mark wandered up with a sandwich in his hand. "Showing off pictures of my goddaughter?"

"Goddaughter?" Ben was baffled.

"Mark's my neighbor and rescuer the day Mia was born." Cate laughed.

"Interesting." Ben sat back, prepared to hear the story.

"Well, I drove Cate and the boys to the hospital when she was in labor," Mark boasted, taking a seat beside Cate. "Let's say it was in the nick of time."

"Mark's also one of the first people I met when I came out to L.A.," Cate added.

"Sweet Cate was a mere house-sitter in those days. Now she owns the place," Mark clowned.

Cate's script was spread out on her desk next to the bed. She munched absentmindedly on a Vienna hot dog when her phone rang.

"Kyle, hi! Gosh, I miss you." She lowered herself to the bed.

"Hi, sweetheart. How's the shoot?" Kyle's voice was upbeat.

"It's great. It's such a fun project. I'm glad I agreed to do it. I should wrap by the end of the week. How's yours?" She was so delighted to be talking to him instead of his voicemail.

Kyle complained, "We've had some issues."

"Technical difficulties?" She sulked. "Will you be behind schedule?"

"No, we'll catch up."

She was busting to share an idea. "I was wondering … instead of flying straight home from Chicago, I could fly to Phoenix and have a nice weekend with you. Mom probably wouldn't mind watching the kids for a couple of extra days. What do you think? I wouldn't be in the way, would I?"

"No, of course not. Cate, that'd be wonderful. I can get Ruth to coordinate it for you in the morning." Kyle sounded relieved.

"Terrific. I'm excited to see you." Cate laid back on her pillow.

"Me too. I miss you, honey."

"I love you. See you soon." Cate jumped back up and finished the last of her hot dog.

Chapter 12
Valley of the Sun

he driver left Cate and her bags at the security entrance. When she couldn't provide a badge, the officer inspected her driver's license, not seeming to recognize her name. *Catherine Leigh Weston.* And she was not on the list. Glaring at her suspiciously, he made several walkie-talkie communiqués until he eventually contacted Ruth. Cate was used to safety measures on productions, but this seemed excessive.

Ruth pulled up in an electric cart.

"Cate, I'm sorry about the confusion. I put your name on the list this morning." Ruth asked for the officer's clipboard and exhaled forcefully. "This is yesterday's sheet," she chided.

Ruth squeezed Cate's arm. "The set's locked down, so security's tight."

"Why?" Cate scanned the area, concerned.

"No need to worry. It's a big city." Ruth picked up one bag. "Kyle's so happy you're here. It's all he's talked about. He's shooting the final scene for today."

Cate carried the other bag and put it in the electric cart.

Lightning was an action-suspense drama with lots of car chases and explosions. The scene being shot called for Kyle to jump from a window and chase the bad guy across traffic, bullets flying. Kyle did most of his stunts, even though he had a stunt double. A downtown section of Central Avenue, the main thoroughfare in Phoenix, had been blocked off for a short period. The scene needed to be shot quickly.

After the wrap, Kyle spoke to the director for an extended period. Cate resigned herself to the long wait. She had a sick feeling that coming to the shoot might have been a mistake. Perhaps Cate was doing what Kyle's past girlfriend, Veronica, had done, invading his workspace. He was exceedingly focused when he worked, which she respected. Had her loneliness gotten the better of her?

When he did come over to her, he apologized distractedly.

"Cate, I'm sorry. Let's get to the suite." Giving her a fleeting kiss, scarcely making contact, he pulled her by the hand. They transferred her bags to Kyle's rental car and went to his hotel. He didn't speak the whole way. His distance troubled her.

Still silent, he led her to the suite and locked the door behind them. Cate crossed to the couch, bewildered.

"Kyle, this is what it must feel like to be a movie star groupie who made it into the star's suite to have sex. Yay!" She sarcastically put two thumbs up.

"It's been a rough time. Crazy stuff's happening," he said, sitting beside her. "I missed you so much."

"I was beginning to wonder if I shouldn't have come."

"No, no … I'm so glad you're here." He flashed a slight grin and then slumped down, appearing hindered by the words he held back.

"What's going on, Kyle?" She turned sideways to face him.

He snatched a recent tabloid from the coffee table and handed it to her. On the cover was a picture of Cate at Wrigley Field with a handsome young Cubs ballplayer, signing the foul ball he had hit. The caption read, *Cate's Playing Foul with Kyle.*

"Kyle, I told you, the production team went to the game. It was for publicity. The cast had their pictures taken with different players. I'm guessing mine was the story the tabloids could best twist."

"I know. I'm just tired of our life being invaded for the public's entertainment."

Cate took a deep breath and again began to broach the subject. "Kyle, I know you love this work, your career … maybe you … we could take a break." She moved closer to him. "The kids are growing up. It'd be wonderful to simply be a family for a while. One day, we're going to wake up, and they'll be gone, living their own lives."

"*Cats in the Cradle*," Kyle stated.

"Harry Chapin," she said with a knowing smile. "Let's not attach a sad memory to our car karaoke game, okay?"

Although he heard Cate's words, he had a withdrawn look on his face.

"Kyle, I think more's bothering you than this." She held up the paper. "Why don't you tell me what it is? Is it the shoot?"

He didn't answer.

"So, if it's not the shoot," she asked, "what is it? Does it have something to do with the increased security?"

He sat up tersely. His look was piercing. Then tenderly, he kissed her, becoming more ardent, not responding to her question. He began to unbutton her blouse, leaving the couch to walk backward into the bedroom. Cate knew she was not getting an answer, not tonight.

The desert beige spotted with saguaros and paloverde green was awash as one rounded the bend of a large mountain. Suddenly, the fiery magnificence of the red rocks appeared as if God haphazardly dropped them there from the sky for your pleasure. It was breathtaking, and Cate fell in love with Sedona's grandeur.

The Native American spirit blew across the land, filling the brilliance of the Canyon, which wound down into the red rocks. Cate and Kyle took advantage of his two days of downtime for this brief but peaceful trip. Sightseeing everything Sedona and its surrounding areas offered, they indulged in homemade fudge and cooling margaritas.

The sun was low in the sky, transforming into a majestic sunset. As they sat on the winding trail of Bell Rock, the red dust covering them like a baptism, Kyle looked seriously at Cate.

"Some of my fans can be a little extreme," he said quietly.

Cate gaped at him, stunned he was finally opening up to her.

"Anyway, the one who sent me the tabloid I showed you had a note attached to it," he disclosed.

"What did it say?" Cate yanked her baseball cap lower over her eyes, the sun blindingly reflecting off of Courthouse Rock.

"*She's no good. She'll never love you like I do.* It was signed by someone named Molly."

53

"Ooh, honey, that's creepy." Cate cringed while Kyle shrugged it off.

"But she's not the only one. You must have had other strange fans."

"Yeah, some a little enthusiastic." His expression was severe and unyielding.

"Is this the first contact from Molly?"

"Not sure. I get so many. Nothing to worry about, though." He glanced away. Cate's gut told her something was off. She drifted back to her impulsive visit to his office—the thick folder and the bits of heated words. If there was nothing to worry about, why the increased security? Was he thinking he was protecting her?

"Do you know anything about her?" She stared gravely at him.

"Return address is somewhere in Northern California. It's not a big deal. It's been happening for years with lots of fans."

Cate was agitated. "Do we need to do something?"

"We've increased security on the shoot. Like I said, I'm not worried."

His attitude belied his words, Cate felt.

"And for the family?" Cate took Kyle's hand and held it warmly.

"Hell, no. The professionals assured me there's no danger, a harmless crush. It's part of being a celebrity."

By Cate's definition, this was not a crush but a borderline obsession.

"We could take a break at the ranch for a while to avoid the paparazzi." Her heart was beating rapidly.

"We can't stop working, Catie." He held her face gently, "It'll be okay. I promise that I won't let anything hurt you or the kids."

Staring at the ground, Cate hid her trepidation. It was so tranquil gazing across the range. She wished they could shun returning to the madness of Los Angeles.

Trekking down the side of the rock, Kyle grasped Cate's hand, pulling her to a stop.

"Stay." Kyle implored.

"Stay? In Sedona?" She stared at him oddly.

"No, on location with me." His urgency was apparent.

"Honey, the kids, my mom. I need to get back." Cate was torn.

"Please," he begged. "I need you, Catie."

She examined his eyes, filled with anxiety—a look she had not seen before from him.

54

"All right. I'll figure it out." They hiked down the mountain, and she nudged him friskily. "I guess I can be a movie star groupie for a while."

"No, just my best friend." He gave her a soft kiss. "With benefits."

Chapter 13
Old South

The seasons flowed into the early summer when Robbie spent three weeks in Montgomery with Alex and Kara. Cate loathed this annual event. Robbie always returned a little aloof, and it would be a few days before he would revert to his usual sweet self.

Cate never pried but was convinced Alex made derogatory remarks which caused Robbie to put up walls, barring his mixed-up feelings. This trip must have been a difficult one because Robbie was closed off.

The house had an appetizing aroma from tonight's dinner simmering on the stove. Cate was making her fabulous chili recipe. Scott was keeping an eye on Mia trying to dress Oakley in a bonnet, and Robbie stared off at the surf from the opened double-deck doors, his back to everyone. Kyle was out of town on a publicity tour.

Cate tried to draw Robbie's responsiveness back to the family. "So, Robbie, did you have a good time in Alabama? How are they doing? Is Kara still working at Alex's company?"

"It was all right," he mumbled, Cate straining to hear.

"What's that?"

"I said it was bad," Robbie yelled in anger.

"Bad?" Cate was upset. "What do you mean bad?"

Scott swung around after he heard Robbie's statement and stared at him.

"He lost his job, okay?" Robbie slammed the deck doors closed. "And he's living in an apartment now."

Cate turned down the burner on the range and walked into the living room. "Oh, honey, I'm sorry."

"Sure you are," Robbie said curtly.

"Yes, of course I am. I wish Alex well."

"Right," he said sarcastically.

"What?"

"Nothing."

Cate had to salvage the discussion. "Living in an apartment? Did they sell their house?"

"No! It was foreclosed!" Robbie snapped, stomping out of the room. Startled anxiety settled in Cate's eyes.

Scott set down his book. "I'll go," he assured her, walking toward Robbie's room.

The door creaked open.

"Go away," Robbie growled with his back to the door, fully expecting it was his mother.

"Let's go for a walk," Scott advised, weathering Robbie's hostility.

Glancing over his shoulder, Robbie's expression implored Scott. He needed his brother.

They stopped at a bench with a scenic view of the beach. Scott straddled the top of it, enjoying the sunlight. Robbie sat next to his brother, sullen and withdrawn.

"You want to talk about what happened in Alabama?"

"I got off the plane, and my dad was a wreck," Robbie hissed. "He lost his job, lost his house. Kara ran off with some dude her own age. He blames Mom for everything." Robbie tugged at a loose thread from his sneakers.

"Mom? Why Mom? They've been divorced for years." Scott removed his phone from his pocket when he felt it vibrate, clicking it off and setting it on the bench.

"I don't know. He made me listen to every problem they ever had during their marriage. Way too personal." Robbie balked. "He told me a bunch of stuff about Mom and Dad … you know that Mom cheated with Dad when she was still married to my father."

"Shit, he said those things? That's messed up."

Robbie was red with anger, fighting the tears welling up inside. "Is any of it true, Scott?" He looked Scott in the eye. "About Mom and Dad?"

"Hell, no! We were there. You may have been too young to remember." Scott met Robbie's glare. "But I do. Mom and Dad were friends, just friends. They had nothing to do with it. Your father's probably to blame and won't admit it."

Behind them, on the Pacific Coast Highway, traffic started to pick up. The noisy congestion distracted from the waves crashing on the shore.

Robbie shook his head, becoming adrift in his turmoil.

"Well, he's struggling now. He's lost everything. He even has to, um, what is it … bankrupt?" Robbie grappled with explaining, slowly fidgeting with his phone. "I have to help him."

Scott frowned. "Rob, you didn't tell him about your trust, did you?"

"Yes. Why?"

"Did he ask for money?"

"I don't think he did. I offered." Robbie flipped his phone over and over again, which was getting on Scott's nerves.

"Did he accept?"

"I'm not sure." Robbie fixed his sight on the surf, thinking hard. "He thanked me."

"Rob, the trusts are for us to go to college and whatever else we need. Mom and Dad wouldn't be thrilled that you're giving away your money." Scott grabbed Robbie's cell phone and set it beside his phone on the bench.

"It's a loan." Robbie pounded his fist on top of the bench in frustration. "Scott, I've got to help my dad. Mom won't. He says she doesn't want him happy."

"Well, that's a load of crap." Scott shifted his position to meet Robbie's eyes. "That doesn't even sound like Mom."

Brooding, Robbie rounded his shoulders forward. "You're right. I guess being with him gets me messed up."

"Maybe you shouldn't be." Scott stammered, lifting his hand as if to wave away his words. "Sorry, I know he's your dad."

Robbie ignored Scott's slip, both sitting in silence, staring at the ocean.

"Scott, thank you for … thanks."

"Hey, I'm your brother, Rob."

After a few minutes, Scott shook Robbie's shoulder and picked up their phones.

"C'mon, let's go home. I'm hungry. That chili smelled good."

The house was empty. Scott opened the front door and stepped in, calling out to their mother. Robbie followed Scott into the living room.

"I need to write Mom a letter, Scott," he huffed.

"Well, let's find everyone first."

Robbie's cell phone began to ring. Glancing at the screen, he looked up nervously to Scott, "It's my dad. I don't want to talk to him."

"No, Rob, you should answer. Just act normal. But don't make any promises about money."

"Hi, Dad," Robbie answered. "Just talkin' with Scott … no, nothing special."

Scott indicated to Robbie that he spotted their mother on the beach through the large picture window. Scott exited through the deck doors, leaving Robbie alone to finish his phone call.

"Hey, Mom," Scott hollered to Cate, catching up with her playing with Mia and Oakley on the beach. Mia had her bucket full of sand, and Oakley was chasing waves.

"Hi, sweetie. Mia and I decided we'd watch the sunset before dinner. So, what's Robbie doing?" Cate rose and walked over to him.

"Alex just called. Then, Robbie's going to write you an apology letter."

"Seriously?" Cate brushed the sand off her hands.

"Yeah, he feels bad he spoke to you the way he did. He had a pretty miserable time in Alabama."

"So, what happened, or would it be violating brother-brother confidentiality to share with me?"

"No, Robbie doesn't mind. Alex is divorced."

"What? When did that happen?" Cate's eyes widened with shock.

"His wife left him for some younger guy."

Well, that's karma, Cate thought, trying to conceal the slight, unexpected twinge of self-satisfaction coming over her.

"Anyway," Scott continued, "when Robbie got there, Alex was raging this was all your fault."

"My fault?" Cate backed away, stunned and angry. "How is it my fault?"

Scott dragged his foot across the top of the sand, leveling it. "Alex is saying horrible stuff about you and Dad. Robbie's caught in the middle hearing this garbage."

"That man could never take responsibility for his own life. He has no right to make Robbie his crying shoulder."

"I don't think it's the only thing he is." Scott stooped down beside Mia to help with her sandcastle.

"What do you mean?" Disquiet flushed Cate's face.

"Ah, nothing. Never mind." Scott stood up. "I'm starving. Is dinner ready?"

"It's been waiting on you two," she smiled.

Scott picked up Mia's bucket. "Hey, Mia, race you to the deck."

Little Mia took off running. Scott picked her up by the waist and ran with her while she giggled hysterically, pretending she was flying with her arms outstretched.

"Oakley, c'mon, let's go," Cate yelled. Oakley bolted past the three of them and plowed up the stairs to the deck.

Scott was such an astonishing young man, Cate reflected. Hard to believe he was almost fifteen. And the older he became, the more he assumed Kyle's best qualities.

Chapter 14
Fields of Gold

"Here, pick. Cowboy hat or baseball cap?"

Kyle wandered over, carrying Mia. "I see you're sporting western garb," he tapped the brim of her hat. Then, taking the cowboy hat she extended, he placed it on his head and the baseball cap on Mia's, who summarily tore it off and threw it to the ground.

"Nostalgia swept over me today," Cate said to Kyle. "Being back at the ranch, basking in the memories of *Sunset Rise* … Mia, angel, please pick up the baseball cap and see if one of your brothers wants to wear it, okay?"

Kyle gave his daughter a big kiss on the cheek and set her down. Mia picked up the cap, took two steps, dropped it again, and ran to her brothers, giggling. Cate rolled her eyes at Kyle, who picked up the hat with a grin and brought it to the blanket to sit next to Cate. Lumbering over, Oakley flopped between Cate and Kyle, shoving them apart.

"Hey, you," Kyle jokingly scolded.

"He knows when to make his move," Cate baby talked Oakley as he wiggled and wagged his way in both of their faces. "He loves me so …"

"Loves me more," Kyle laughed, attempting to bear hug the rambunctious pup who jumped up and plopped down hard onto Kyle's lap.

"Ow, Oakley," he winced in pain.

"Oh, honey, you okay?" Cate tried to suppress her snicker as she moved Oakley off Kyle and back between them, scratching between

Oakley's ears. Kyle followed her lead, slowly petting Oakley on his chest.

"Good boy," Cate gently spoke. "Oakley, go watch Mia for me."

The dog jumped up obediently, concentrating on Cate's expression, gave a muffled bark, and ran to Mia.

"Smart dog," smiled Kyle, brushing grass off the blanket. "He understands everything."

"Hey, boys," Cate called. "Keep an eye on your sister, please."

"Sure, Mom," Scott yelled as Robbie lifted Mia onto Oakley's back.

"Robbie, please don't do that! The poor dog's not a horse. Thank you."

Cate turned to Kyle. "Mia is three and thinks she's six. Robbie is thirteen and can act like he's seven. And then there's Scott … fifteen going on thirty."

"So, how old are the two of us?" Kyle temptingly asked.

"Some days, I feel eighteen again." She peeked up seductively, "Which would make you twenty-four."

"That *would* be interesting," Kyle pondered in his sexiest voice.

"Never would've happened. My brother was super protective. Remember the rock concerts? I was so innocent, incredibly naïve. He would never have let you within a mile of me."

"Probably a good call on his part," Kyle joked.

Cate and Kyle silently took in the entire scene of the blissful day. Suddenly, Kyle started to laugh.

"What?" Cate asked with a chuckle.

"Look at us," said Kyle. "We're so normal."

"Normal?"

"Happy."

"Yes, very."

The *awareness* struck him. "This is the family I always pictured."

After a spell, Kyle rested his head on her lap, shifting the hat over his face.

"As much as I love our time with the kids, being alone, the two of us, like we did for our fifth anniversary, was wonderful."

"Oh, the Sicilian villa on the Mediterranean … heavenly!"

He raised his hat a bit and slyly squinted at her. "Not exactly what I meant, beautiful woman."

Putting on her hat and with a finger to her lips, Cate concentrated hard on interpreting the exact phrasing. She cleared her throat. "Mi piace fare l'amore con te."

Sitting in front of her, hat brim to hat brim, Kyle applauded. "Molto bene. Anch'io, amore mio. Ti amo, Catie." He kissed her.

"Ti amo, Kyle."

He adjusted both of their hats. "I always wanted to star in a spaghetti western."

"Si." She returned his kiss.

The cheery noise of the kids playing along with Oakley's animated barks drifted into their conversation.

"I'm going to get a book to read," she said. "Do you need anything?"

"Just you."

Cate smiled and rose, sauntering back to the house and into the library. She surveyed the room, passing the golden Oscar on the fireplace mantel to the family photos on the center bookshelf. Kyle wandered into the room.

Through the open window, they watched the kids. Mia was shrugging her shoulders at Robbie, flaunting a baby-doll smile. Her cuteness was disarming.

"She has you boys wrapped around her little finger," Cate pronounced.

"And she knows it," Kyle grinned.

Cate was amused, her hands on her hips. "I never had that talent."

"You sure about that?" Kyle said in a husky voice, standing behind and lacing his arms beneath hers. Cate melted into his caress.

"Two becoming one," she sighed, reaching to straighten the rope of dried flowers draped behind the photos.

Kyle gave her another kiss. "I will never get tired of your lips," he said softly.

"*Give me a kiss to build a dream on,*" Cate sang. "*My imagination will thrive upon that kiss.*"

"Louis Armstrong!" Kyle searched his memory, "Where did I hear that recently?"

"Two nights ago. Family movie night, the DVD of *Sleepless in Seattle*. It's in the movie."

"That's right. How's the last part go?"

"*Sweetheart, I ask no more than this, a kiss to build a dream on.*"

"Yes, ma'am." Kyle pulled her in close and kissed her longingly again.

Kyle had followed Cate into the house for a reason. He needed the right moment … this was it.

"Catie, not to change the subject," Kyle began, "but I want to talk to you about something. It's been a while since we shared the screen. I miss working with you."

"We had a little distraction." Cate pointed at Mia's photo on the bookshelf.

"Yes, we did." He hesitated, hunting for persuasive words. "A script came across my desk. It's excellent. There's a part. It's the lead, female lead. It's yours. You're my first and only choice, Cate Leigh. It's the right role for you. It's Oscar-worthy."

Cate froze. "It sounds challenging."

"You're ready. You can do this."

"Honestly?"

"Without a doubt." Kyle could hear the reluctance in Cate's voice, and he gently squeezed her shoulder.

"Leads carry the film. I've never carried a film." Her voice strained.

"We're a team, Cate. We do it together. It's us."

She glanced out the window.

"It's a demanding role," he persisted, "but I've not seen a female character this complex in years."

"Kyle, I do supporting roles. Quirky comedic characters."

"It's perfect for you. For both of us. You can do this role blindfolded."

"Kyle, I …?"

He held her hands.

"Trust me. We go into production in late April."

"Kyle, that's a little over a month from now. It's too soon. I can't. The kids …" Cate seemed rattled.

"I've already talked to your mom. She's happy to stay with them while we're on location." He touched her chin. "Cate, I believe in you. It would be nice to have a matching Oscar on the mantel."

"All I ever wanted was to be a working actor. You're the star." Her gaze met his.

"And all I ever wanted was you." Kyle gently tugged her hand, drew

64

her to him, and kissed her tenderly. "I love you. Always have, always will." He breathed in her perfumed scent; the mood fractured by a commotion occurring outside. Oakley had jumped into the lake, eventually shaking off water and mud all over the kids.

Scott yelled, "Stop, Oakley!"

Robbie shouted, "Yuck."

Mia screamed, "Mommy!"

Kyle pressed his forehead against Cate's. "To be continued."

"You're such a tease," she toyed.

Chapter 15
The Labyrinth

Mother was dead. Good riddance, Molly gloated to herself, clearing her last lunch table to set up for the dinner crowd.

Molly stared out the window at the busy street, recalling the week before when she entered her apartment after work to find Marilyn Lambert sprawled on the kitchen floor, a broken plate full of food splattered everywhere. The paramedics said it appeared Molly's mother had mixed excessive alcohol consumption with painkillers and accidentally overdosed. It was such good news for Molly, except for the mess Marilyn left behind. It figures, judged Molly. Mother was always leaving messes for Molly to clean up.

A distant recollection crossed her senses. She must have been three years old. Mother and Father were yelling in the kitchen. It was a terrible fight, enflaming her mother's mercurial temper to the breaking point. Molly crawled out of bed and peeked around the corner of the doorway.

"You're not a man," Marilyn taunted Molly's dear father. "You're nothing but a worthless piece of shit. Get out!"

And yet, through all the years, her mother had insisted her husband had abandoned them because of Molly. It was the little girl who drove her father away. That was Molly's talent, Marilyn had snidely commented over and over … driving men away.

Molly's once attractive mother indulged in too much booze and brought home strange men to deaden her loneliness. Some men would crawl into a teenage Molly's bed when Marilyn had passed out in the other room. If Mother knew, she certainly didn't care.

Too drunk to work and feigning injury, Marilyn Lambert became hardened, ugly, and hostile. Molly heard the echoes of her mother's relentlessly berating, her repulsive remarks, always predicting Molly would never find someone to love her.

Molly detested caring for her vile mother. The only benefit Molly gathered was Marilyn's large disability check, easing the burden of Molly having to support herself and the woman who despised her.

Demoralized and broken, Molly ran to her room every night, slammed the door, and paged through her collection of tabloid magazines. It became her ritual, lost in the world of glamorous celebrity.

Molly took a deep breath, again picturing that glorious event when she found the body.

"I'm free," she had joyfully shouted. "You're dead. I'm alive."

"I'm sorry about your mom."

The daydream was broken, interrupted by the new waitress. "I understand she'd been sick for a long time," Sara attempted to empathize. "That's rough."

"She wasn't much of a mother," Molly said coldly, glaring at the intruder.

"Oh." Sara didn't know how to respond. Looking away, she changed the subject. "So, what are you doing tonight?"

Molly resented this annoying girl, always trying to engage her in conversation, bubbling and affable. Leave me alone, Molly's mind wailed.

"Well, a group of my friends are meeting me at this new club which is supposed to be really cool. Want to come along? It might be good to get out."

"Can't. There's a Kyle Weston film marathon starting tonight."

"I heard you met Kyle Weston when he was in town filming that movie a few years ago. What was it called?"

"*Devised*," Molly crowed, her face gleaming. There was nothing she loved more than talking about her fella. She pointed at the front table near the window. "I served him at the table right there three times while he was filming for all those months."

"What was he like?"

"He was the best person I've ever met." Her eyes softened with affection. "He was considerate, outgoing, and terribly generous. The biggest tips of my life. I think he liked me because he kept coming in. We had a connection."

Sara peered oddly at Molly. This was more information than she expected.

"Was he alone or with his wife?" Sara casually helped place glasses on the table.

"He wasn't married," Molly barked, slamming down a dish on the table, almost breaking it. Sara backed away.

"Okay. Um, I need to go. See you tomorrow." Sara set down a final glass, turned quickly, and walked to the kitchen.

Of course, Sara wouldn't understand, brooded Molly. No one did. Kyle must have been attracted to Molly. He kept coming back to the restaurant. Yes, it was near the film set and his hotel, but still, he kept coming in. So what if Molly persuaded the hostess to seat him in her section every time. He never complained. He acted surprised … pleasantly. And he wasn't merely friendly and polite. He flirted with her. Molly was sure of that.

Molly rushed home. She had to dodge the brash neighbor walking his two large, intimidating dogs. She wasn't sure what terrorized her more, the chatty man or his dogs sniffing her. When Molly spotted him near her apartment, she shuffled her keys wildly to locate the right one, nearly dropping them. Once inside, she bolted the door behind her.

In the dark dwelling, the curtains allowed a singular stream of light. It landed on a poster of Kyle in *Devised*. As always, she stared at the picture, inviting his presence to overtake her body and soul. She entertained the fantasy, Kyle knocking on her door right now, having searched endlessly for her.

Switching on the kitchen light, Molly gazed at a photograph of herself she had found under a pile of junk in her mother's room. Molly's mind drifted into the frozen photo.

Molly recalled the picture was taken outside the theater where she had gone on a date to see a Kyle Weston movie. She was much younger then, with a bright, joyful smile. Bret was kind and so nice to her. She dreamed of running away with him, escaping her mother's clutches. Marilyn resented Molly's happiness and nitpicked everything about Bret, calling him worthless like her father and only using Molly for sex. To prove her point, Marilyn tried to seduce Bret, who refused her in disgust. That only caused Marilyn to spin threats of suicide unless Molly broke up with him. It didn't matter ... Bret never returned.

Molly wished she had a picture of her old boyfriend. She could barely recall his deep blue eyes.

Molly taped her picture on the wall next to her poster of *Devised*. Stroking Kyle's face, she broke out into a lively grin when she noticed it appeared as if they were watching each other.

Molly turned on the sofa lamp and took the new issue of *Movie Inquiry Magazine* from her handbag. Kyle was on the cover with Leigh holding their three-year-old daughter. The headline read: *Kyle's Ladies*. Molly quickly flipped through the magazine to find the article. Slowly, she read about Kyle's forty-eighth birthday party and the Westons' multimillion-dollar beach house.

Looking at the cover photo of Kyle and his so-called family, Molly knew what she had to do. Yanking open the often stuck desk drawer, she pulled out several computer pages filled with photos of her in assorted sizes. She carefully cut out her head from one of the copies and, using a glue stick, affixed it over Leigh's. Yes, it fit perfectly. And, strangely, Kyle looked so much happier. But the child was still there. Wait, considered Molly, this little girl didn't even look that much like Kyle. It probably wasn't even his.

This reminded Molly of something. What was it? She laid her head on the desk and tried to remember ... a distant time ... her parents arguing in the kitchen ... the day Father left ...

"You're nothing but a worthless piece of shit. Get out!"

Suddenly, Marilyn spotted Molly. "What the hell are you doing up?"

Father rushed over to little Molly, picking her up in his arms, "I'll go, but I'm taking Molly with me. I won't leave my daughter with you."

"You're a fool if you believe she's your child," Marilyn sneered.

"Whose is she?" he yelled.

"I don't know, but I sure as hell know she's not yours. Did you forget that job you had out of town? Are you too stupid to do simple math?"

Scrutinizing Molly's features, he shook his head sadly, slowly setting her down. He turned and, without another word, crossed to the door. That was the last time Molly saw her father. Not even so much as a glimpse back ... no birthday cards ... nothing.

Turning her head to look at the little girl on the tabloid cover, Molly grabbed a permanent ink marker. Carefully, she marked out Mia's face.

The cuckoo clock on the wall clucked the hour. Molly settled in to enjoy the company of the man of her dreams. It was time for the Kyle Weston film marathon to begin.

Chapter 16
Piercing Heat

K yle was on the sundeck reading, listening to the waves beyond.

"Kyle, there's a nude scene! Do you expect me to do a nude scene? Have you met me?" Cate stomped up to the chaise. He slid his sunglasses down and glanced up at her.

"There's also violence and foul language. Lots of f-words." He closed the book and set it beside his leg.

"So, I may not say them. That doesn't mean I don't think them."

"Catherine, I'm shocked." He razzed.

"Kyle!" She glared at him.

"Sorry." He chuckled.

Cate furrowed her brow. "We've been married more than five years. You should know I'm ..."

"Extremely shy," he finished.

She placed her finger on the end of her nose. "Ding, ding, ding."

Kyle laughed at her silliness.

"Seriously, how are you expecting me to do this with the world watching?" She frowned.

"Cate, it's a love scene, it's essential to the plot, and the audience won't see anything vital the way it's shot. It'll be more suggestive."

"Anything vital?" Cate waved her hands over her body. "Pretty much all of this is vital, in my opinion. And what about the film crew who will see everything?"

"Closed set, minimal personnel. If it bothers you, you can get a body double."

"Oh." Cate mulled over his proposal, erupting into a smile. "Okay, yes. I could find someone with a better body, right?" She relaxed beside him on the empty chaise. "After all, I'm not a teenager anymore. I'm forty-two years old."

"No one has a better body, sweetheart," he grinned.

"Please …" she mocked.

"Seriously, if you're more comfortable with a double, I think it's a good idea. Lots of actors have a clause in their contracts requiring body doubles." He turned to his side to see her reaction, "Do know, it means I'm doing a nude scene with a strange woman. I've done it on a lot of shoots. I'm quite used to it."

"Oh! Don't go there." With a glint of exasperation, she allowed her amusement to appear.

"Cate, you've always trusted me. Trust me now." Kyle sat up to face her. "This script will push you. I knew the scene might make you a little uncomfortable. It's you and me. I won't let anything happen to you."

"The kids can't come to the movie."

"They can't watch three-quarters of what we've made anyway. If that's the measure of what we do, we'd only be making Disney and Marvel films." He stretched down and picked up his book again, opening the page he left off reading. "We'll hire the body double in case."

"Safety net?" She laid back again, drumming her fingers on the chaise beside her thigh.

"Yeah."

"You're pushing my limits, Kyle Weston." Cate held a reprimanding finger up at him.

"Sorry. Yes, or no?"

"Maybe?" She scrunched her nose.

"Maybe's fine … so how about a little preview?"

She blushed, "You're so naughty."

The wind whipped, drawing Cate to the railing, hearing the surge of white-capped waves crashing to shore. In truth, the script terrified her. It had many elements drastically beyond her comfort level. The brutal opening flashback foreshadowed the complex storyline, the psychological distress of being isolated with the hauntings of some unknown force nearly driving her to madness, reminiscent of *Gas Light*, with most other characters trying to destroy her. Only Kyle's character believed her, shielding her from the town's hostility to his detriment. It ended as violently as it began.

The script's attraction was the depth of character development, a well-crafted plot line with a surprise ending, and a tender love story amid the chaos. It was also blessed to have Rodolfo Reno as director. This year, 2014, he was hailed as a "modern-day visionary in the industry, a true storyteller." He allowed the narrative to play out entirely without interruption, and he shot sequentially. He used multiple cameras to focus on different shot angles, inherently edifying each scene. It allowed actors the freedom to grow with their characters and undergo the tale unfolding the way the audience would experience it.

Cate also had to consider Kyle's unquestionable faith in her. She couldn't let him down. The irony, Cate realized, was if he truly knew her, he'd never consider her for the part. Yes, it was a leap, far surpassing what she had previously done. Cate's fear mounted, sticking in her throat, making it hard to breathe. She roughly shook her head, trying to rid her mind of demons.

Piercing Heat was extremely physical, with explicit violence at the beginning and end of the script. As promised, the director had given Cate the license to experiment with her portrayal of the wealthy Miranda Redman. The role was enlightening, fulfilling, and very hard work.

The dreaded nude scene was long completed, complicated in its vulnerability. All that remained to shoot was the ending, a simple conclusion to the action. Yet, for some reason, Cate was on edge. She didn't know why.

The scenes prior were savage. Cate was seized by the energy of the emotional build-up of the plot. She was fighting for her life, ultimately killing the man in self-defense who had driven her to the brink of insanity. The final scene was with Kyle as Detective Reave Evans. Evans trusted Miranda's innocence and risked everything to prove it.

Cameras began to roll, and sound cued. "And action."

Miranda was led out of the mansion in handcuffs by two police officers.

"What are you doing? She's not under arrest." Evans stormed over to unlock her handcuffs. Miranda was in shock.

"Detective, Mayor Redman said she killed his brother," the first officer replied.

"Self-defense. There're plenty of witnesses." Evans glowered at Mayor Redman, ordering police officers and EMTs around in the background.

Released, Miranda, rubbing her wrists, wandered down to the pavilion to sit on the stoop.

Evans grabbed the officer's arm. "Tell the mayor he's trespassing and has to leave."

Evans crossed over to Miranda and crouched down in front of her. She had a cut above her left brow, and he gently wiped the blood away with his thumb. She was staring remorsefully off into the night.

"You okay?" Evans asked.

Miranda didn't respond.

"Miranda, it's over."

"No, they'll always hate me."

"It doesn't matter what they think." Evans gestured towards the estate. "This is yours now. No one can take it from you. You're free."

"I don't want it. I never wanted any of it. This isn't freedom. It's a prison sentence." Miranda examined the area.

Evans knelt in front of her, "So let it all go. You don't need it." He took her hand. "Sometimes, you just have to walk away."

For Evans, it was his final line. Miranda was to say one word ... "Together." The scene would end, and the movie would wrap.

Cate gazed up at Kyle, frightened. The word didn't leave her lips. Instead, she cried, "What?"

Cate's look begged Kyle. She was off script. She broke. An old nightmare, an old feeling, invaded her. Her mind screamed, "Not again. I can't do this again."

Kyle kept in character, aware something was happening. Cate began to shake. Her expression slowly evolved from hard determination through emotions of betrayal, loss, and hopelessness, her eyes filling with tears. She struggled futilely to keep them from falling.

Rodolfo motioned for the cameras to stay on Cate.

Kyle decided he would repeat his line. "Sometimes, you have to walk away."

Cate raised her trembling hands, placed them on either side of Kyle's face, and joined him on her knees in front of him, her cheeks stained with free-flowing tears. Finally, the words came in desperation.

"Walk with me?" she pleaded.

He lifted each of her hands and kissed her palms. He clasped them together, almost in a prayer position. Opening his arms to her, she fell into his grasp. The scene ended by capturing them kneeling and holding each other, police milling around, flashing blue lights, and the ambulance driving away.

"And cut." There was a silent reverence from all. A couple of the crew wiped their cheeks and cleared their throats. Kyle maintained his embrace of Cate and whispered, "Are you all right?"

She barely nodded. Kyle kissed her cheek.

"My enchanting, Catherine … wonderful," Rodolfo gushed, breaking the silence.

Cate wiped away her leftover tears. "I'm sorry I messed up the line," she said contritely.

"No, Catherine, good change. It worked. Give me a minute."

The makeup artist came over to Cate to touch up her makeup in case there were pickup shots. After a few minutes, it was called.

"Everyone, it's a wrap!" The cast and crew applauded and cheered.

Kyle gently held her arm. "We should go to the suite and rest before the wrap party tonight."

"No, I have to go to the gym and work out. I need to unwind." She shook her hands out as if they were dripping with fire. "I'll tell you what. I'll meet you at the party." She detected his concern. "I'm fine, Kyle. Honest." She rubbed her left arm with her hand, not making eye contact, and hurried to her dressing room to change. Kyle's mind raced to rewind the last few minutes.

The establishment had been rented out for the cast party. No outside patrons were allowed, giving the room a family feel. Waiting for Cate, Kyle fielded endless questions concerning his wife's whereabouts. An hour passed, and his frustration had turned to deep worry.

Alan, the first assistant director, came up to him. "Kyle, I saw Cate outside. She's on her way in." Kyle's relief was enormous, despite still being troubled.

The door opened and flooded the room with fresh, crisp Carmel-by-the-Sea air. Cate's eyes scoured the restaurant to locate Kyle, *Shut Up and Dance* by Walk the Moon beginning to play on the club's sound system. Kyle stood in the middle of the dance floor with a big grin, holding out his hand. Cate set her purse on the front table and rushed to him. When she reached him, he spun her into a swing dance, and the party began, the jovial Cate and Kyle taking center stage.

The bed was cozy, Kyle holding Cate in his arms.

Her performance had been riveting, as if a secret, stolen from within the depths of Cate's soul, became unmasked.

Kyle spoke softly and deliberately, "You had me a little worried. You were so amazing, it was scary. Where did that come from?" Kyle stroked her hair.

"Not sure. I try to stay in the moment. Thank you for working with me." Cate snuggled.

"I'm an actor. Throw a new wrinkle at me, and I better be able to react and stay in character."

"I appreciate it. It was powerful what you did. It kept me going." Cate glimpsed up at him. "Thank you for this. For the script and trusting I could do it."

"You believe in me, and I believe in you. It makes us a great team in everything we do." Kyle kissed her. "Tell the truth, the love scene wasn't that awkward, was it?"

"Yes, it *was*. And so embarrassing. I was worried about how many takes we'd do. But after a while, it became ... oh, no. I shouldn't say this ..." She placed her hands over her face to hide.

"No, Cate, you're not leaving me hanging. What?"

"If I'm honest, it was pretty hot."

"Well, damn," Kyle laughed. "I wasn't expecting to hear that. Maybe easy or even *fun*. But *hot*?"

Cate pulled the covers over her face and slid down. "Oh, don't make me regret telling you. It was because I was with you and not some random actor." She popped out from beneath the covers. "It made all the difference."

"It's nice you're getting over your shyness."

"Just with you." She kissed him, and he rolled her over to her back.

"We could do a reenactment right now."

"Intriguing," Cate lured.

Kyle turned off the light while kissing Cate.

It was a fantastic shoot in stunning Carmel. And this, their last night on location, was an idyllic time muting the challenging experience. Both were fulfilling.

Chapter 17
The Walk

The summer was over. The air carried a chill. Cate readjusted Mia's hat upon her head, the four-year-old bending down to pick up a shimmering unbroken shell.

"Mommy, look."

"Wow. Mia, how pretty. Let's put the shell in your bucket."

Mia did so, and the two roamed along the water, hunting for buried treasures in the sand. Oakley was more interested in a clump of seaweed clustered on the shore.

Cate spotted a flat shell laying delicately on top of the sand. Each wave coming to shore would wash it a little further inland. Mia followed Cate out to scoop it from the sand before the tide snatched it away.

"Mia, this is a sand dollar. I haven't seen one in California in ages."

Mia's eyes were large with awe. She gently placed it in her bucket.

Cate's cell phone rang. "Hi, Tom … It will need to be tomorrow. Mia's school let out early today … Okay, what time?" Mia had left Cate's sight for a second. Cate turned to find her with a stranger crouching in front of her, talking to her. "Tom, I have to go." Cate hung up and ran over.

"Mia!" Cate grasped her child and encountered a woman who gradually stood. She wore a baseball hat under a hoodie, her eyes covered with dark glasses, and her hands hidden in her pockets. It was almost impossible to make out any features.

"Hello," the stranger muttered, "I was admiring your daughter's seashells."

Feeling strangely anxious, Cate studied the intruder's appearance to see if she had a camera and could be paparazzi.

"She looks like you," the woman offered.

Cate scanned the beach. It was deserted except for the three of them.

"Do you live in this area? This part of the beach is private access only."

"I'm staying with friends."

Cate took in every detail of the surroundings. The woman was restlessly adjusting something in her right pocket.

"Well, I'm familiar with everyone who owns here. Who're your friends?" Cate persisted, still combing the beach for people.

"She looks so much like you one might think she didn't have a father." The stranger's tenor sounded ominous.

A cold chill went down Cate's spine at the bizarre remark. She moved Mia to stand behind her. "She does have a father," Cate blurted.

Without taking her eyes off the trespasser, Cate spoke to Mia, grabbing for her hand, "Honey, we need to go." Cate shouted to the dog, "Oakley!"

Oakley's interest in the seaweed waned at hearing Cate's call, and he scurried back. The instant he saw the outsider, his hackles rose, his bark loud and fierce. He stood between the danger and his family in a protective, attack stance. The woman lurched back a few steps and then froze. Distressed Oakley might lunge at the woman, Cate dropped to her knees and held the dog, wrestling with constraining him.

"Sorry, he never behaves this way. He's very gentle. We better go." Oakley fought Cate's restraint as she took hold of his collar and stood up, clutching Mia's hand.

The stranger, motionless, scrutinized Cate hastening Mia and Oakley to the beach house.

Cate locked the doors securely and sank onto the sofa, holding Mia on her lap with Oakley lying across Cate's feet.

She picked up her phone, her hands shaking.

"I need to see you … No, not on the phone. Mia will be with me … Thank you. Be there soon."

"Catherine, how nice to see you. Is this Mia? Oh, my goodness, you're so big." Edward's receptionist, Tina, opened the glass door when they approached. It was an imposing reception area even for a Beverly Hills law firm. "Edward will be out momentarily. Is it all right if I entertain Miss Mia in the conference room? We have cable."

"Thank you, Tina." Cate knelt in front of Mia. "Mommy's going to have a quick chat with Uncle Ed."

"Okay, can I watch *Winnie the Pooh*?"

"Sure, Mia," Tina said and led Mia to another room.

Edward's office was a throwback to the old studio execs of the '50's elegance. It was full of fantastic eclectic, masculine, and costly artwork. Edward's taste was refined. The Remington always impressed Cate.

"So, what couldn't you tell me over the phone?" He sat behind his large desk, and Cate sat in the chair across from him.

"Nothing good."

Cate relayed the episode to Edward. He listened, an experienced attorney evaluating the merits of the case.

"Did you tell Kyle?"

"No, I'd rather not. Not until I'm sure there's a need to worry." She was on the edge of her seat. "Kyle went through a disturbing incident a couple of years ago, and it seemed to throw him. He's been on a career-high the last few months, and I don't want to spoil it unless it's absolutely necessary. That's why I'm coming to you. You retain investigators, don't you?"

"Yes, I do. If you're getting an investigator involved, you need to hire security." Edward reclined back in his oversized chair, watching her jittery actions.

"Not yet. I need more information to see if we have a problem. If we do, then I'll do anything I can to protect my children and make sure they're safe."

Edward rose, stepped over to Cate, took her hand, and guided her to sit down on the couch beside him.

"I need my sister safe," he said sternly. "I'll make some inquiries. The first one will be to your management team to see if they're aware of any unusual fans. I should contact Ruth since she's your P.R. manager."

"You can't. She'd tell Kyle."

"You're making this difficult, Catherine. Okay, I'll get the investigator on it. Now can I go steal a hug from my precious niece?"

"Yes. Thank you, Ed." Cate welcomed a degree of relief.

It was the second trip to Edward's office in a week. She eyed a picture of Edward and Beverly on his end table by the couch.

"Are you two getting serious, Brother?"

"We're good together," he said. "It's all your fault."

"My fault?"

"You and Kyle make it look so easy. You inspired me to develop a good relationship with the right woman." Edward picked up some files and strolled to the couch beside her.

"I always told you it's important to be with someone who you shared a common interest."

"You did, didn't you? Before I married Valerie. I should have listened to my kid sister." Edward set the files beside him.

"Yes, but you have beautiful Emily to show for it. So, it wasn't a total mistake." She fiddled with his golden gavel award next to the photo on the table.

"Put that down," he scolded.

"Sorry," she set it down carefully. "So, I hope you have news. I can't keep saying I have another manicure appointment."

"Well, your nails do look nice." Edward presented a folder to Cate. "They found nothing. The report determined it was harmless. There's nothing there."

Cate roughly paged through the file. "Are you sure? My gut told me something was off. And Oakley, he typically loves everybody. He was going to tear her apart."

"I'm telling you what my investigator found. Nothing." Edward hoisted another thick report and handed it to her. "However, I did uncover some information for you about the prior incident you mentioned that occurred two years ago in Phoenix."

Cate scooted up to peruse the second document.

"Fall of 2012," Edward pinpointed. "During that time, Kyle was receiving peculiar communications from a fan, Molly Lambert. It shook him enough to explore getting the family security. Don't be too alarmed, though. It's not the first time he has had to do that."

"What happened?"

"Nothing. The threat went away. It always does. It seemed to stop after Phoenix. Nothing that we could find these last couple of years."

"And you don't think this is related?" Cate fretfully turned the pages of the report.

Edward reached out and held her hand. "What I believe is you and Kyle live as if you're everyday folks and you're not. I've been convinced you've needed more security for a long time, more than electric gates and security systems. You need personnel."

"Bodyguards? Ed, I'd feel like I was living in a gilded cage. What kind of life is that for any of us?"

"The term is personal security," he stated judiciously, "and it's a life."

"You're worried?" She searched his demeanor.

"No, the investigator said there's no evidence of a threat. But I'm your brother, and I care."

"So?"

"Don't upset yourself, but start being more aware of your surroundings." He kissed her cheek.

"Thank you." She hugged him, "I appreciate what you did."

"Anytime, Sis."

"Just resume living an ordinary, peaceful life," Cate said softly to herself as she left the office. Still, she had a nagging suspicion there was more to this story than what was found.

Chapter 18
Uncle Oscar

obbie gently roused Kyle from a sound sleep. "Dad."

"What is it, Rob?" Kyle squinted, the blinding hall light flooding his bedroom.

Robbie's silhouette was all that was distinguishable in the light. "It's Mom. She and Mia and Oakley are out on the beach dancing."

"What? What time is it?" Kyle woke slowly.

"A little after six. The sun's rising."

"Why are they out there?" Kyle glanced at Cate's empty side of the bed.

"I don't know. They're having fun, though."

"I'll get dressed. You get dressed too." Kyle groaned, his feet hitting the floor.

Cate picked up Mia and whirled her around, squealing with nonstop laughter while the languidly brightening dawn peeked through the spaces between the line of beach houses. They danced to Madonna's *Holiday*, playing on Cate's phone. Oakley rolled in the sand.

Quietly, Kyle and Robbie walked from the beach house.

"Girls, having fun?"

"Yay, Daddy," Mia shrieked, running to jump into Kyle's arms.

Cate kept dancing, carried away by the music, not addressing the distraction.

"Kyle, Robbie, come dance with us," she laughed. "We're celebrating!"

"Everything okay?" Kyle cautiously queried.

"Okay? It's spectacular!" Cate glowed with energy. "I'm nominated for an Oscar."

Giving Mia a peck on her cheek and handing her to Robbie, Kyle sprinted to Cate.

"Catie, how incredible! Best Actress?"

"Best Actress!" Her entire being vibrated with joy.

"I'm so proud of you." He snapped up Cate and whirled her as she had with Mia. Robbie set Mia down and held her hand, Mia hopping up and down.

"I'm not surprised. You were amazing. I knew you'd be nominated."

"I'm so happy," she screamed above the music and waves, giddy with excitement.

Robbie hugged his mother. "Mom, you're the greatest movie star in the world … well, Dad too …"

As usual, Mark was out walking his dog along the beach. Oakley leaped from the sand to greet Roxy.

"Hey, Cate. I heard," grinned Mark. "Congratulations!" Mark walked on, whistling to Roxy, who refused to stop playing with Oakley.

"Thanks, Mark," called Cate. "Oakley, come here. Roxy has to go."

Robbie picked up Cate's phone to change the music, a curious look on his face.

"Mom, your phone's going nuts. You have at least ten missed calls and all kinds of texts."

Cate reached out for the phone, Kyle snatching it away.

"Oh, no. Not until after we celebrate," he said, scrolling through Cate's playlist for the perfect song.

"Yes," he smiled. "*Do You Believe in Magic?*"

"Lovin' Spoonful," she laughed. "And yes, I do."

"May I have this dance, milady?" He extended his hand.

"Of course, kind sir." She was charmed, spinning into his arms.

Cate and Kyle did a swing while Robbie and Mia chased the waves with Oakley. The light from the sun spread across the sand, spotlighting the festivities. Kyle scooped Mia up and twirled her in the air. Cate danced with Robbie while Oakley bounced up and down, barking for attention. The paparazzi had their cover photo.

Making their way past cheering fans and the line of press on the red carpet, Cate and Kyle were ushered to their front row seats.

"This isn't happening," Cate mumbled, her knees nearly buckling.

Kyle angled closer to her. "What did you say, sweetheart?"

Cate's body was beginning to betray the nervousness she had gallantly concealed. Kyle gently squeezed her hand. It was cold and trembling. "Cate, it's all right. I'm here," he winked with a wise grin. "Deep breath ... this is fun."

She clutched Kyle's arm, and he kissed her softly.

Piercing Heat was up for several awards, including Best Screenplay. As Rodolfo Reno walked to the stage to accept the Oscar for Best Director, Cate's breathing became shallow with tension, her concentration wandering, worried about the next presentation ... Best Actress.

Cate's attention was jerked back when Rodolfo said, "I especially want to thank our producer and star, Kyle Weston. He's as brilliant behind the camera as in front." Rodolfo placed his hand over his heart. "And to the lovely and talented Catherine Leigh, my heart is full! Thank you." Rodolfo, every bit Italian, blew her a kiss from the stage. Cate and Kyle felt honored.

The time had come ...

"And the Oscar for Best Actress goes to ... Catherine Leigh for *Piercing Heat*."

Cate's mind went fuzzy, unable to comprehend what she was hearing. Kyle's touch brought her back to the present, happily whispering that she needed to stand and go to the stage. Still dazed but overwhelmingly ecstatic, Cate approached the microphone. She scanned the audience with a palliative exhale, waiting for the applause to die down.

"This is my childhood fantasy, and there are so many people to thank." She held up the Oscar and studied its curves, holding back her joyous tears. She began her litany of appreciation to the appropriate people, highlighting her children, brother, and mother.

"There is one more person," Cate flushed, the audience wildly hooting, laughing, and clapping in anticipation. "Oh, you know who

I'm talking about," she giggled, to even louder cheers. She waited for the uproar to simmer, her beautiful smile having already captured the elated crowd. "I want to thank my best friend, who also happens to be my incredible husband, Kyle Weston." More applause, Cate was looking directly at Kyle. "Without you, none of this could be possible. You gave me the opportunity, the encouragement, and the love to create a new dream. I love you forever."

As Cate was led backstage to the interview room, she paused at a large monitor, knowing the final award was being presented.

"And the Oscar goes to *Piercing Heat*."

Kyle and the production team were jubilant, a large parade to the podium.

"Let's get you back to the stage," smiled Cate's escort.

Chapter 19
Crashing

olly stared at the mirror. Dark circles under her eyes, stark against her pale skin … she looked so much thinner. Opening her apartment door, Molly carefully glanced both ways, locking the door behind her. After scoping out the area, she ran down the walkway.

"Lambert," yelled a harsh voice.

Molly was trapped. The apartment owner stood in her pathway, fury in his eyes.

"Can't talk, Mr. Smith. I'm late for work."

"Lambert, you're four months behind," he bellowed, spraying spittle with each word. "And don't blame it on your mother's death again. That was almost three years ago."

"I know, I'm sorry," she recoiled, wiping the spit from her cheek and nose. "But, without her disability check, it's been difficult."

"I don't care about your financial problems. If I don't get your rent check today, you're out. I have to eat too, you know."

"Sorry, I have to go." She scooted around him and ran to her car.

"No excuses," he hollered. "Today, understand?"

The kitchen help was frenetically attempting to keep up with the demand. Dishware clanging, fire searing on the enormous stove, the noise and clatter topping the voices calling orders. Despite the busy lunch crowd, Molly stole a minute at her kitchen locker to skim the latest issue of *Movie Inquiry*. She would read it thoroughly after work. She flipped to the centerfold. It was still there. Catherine Leigh, hanging all over Kyle while all the *Piercing Heat* bigwigs stood on stage pawing over the Best Picture Oscar. And there she was again on the next page, holding up the statue with that painted smile of hers. The caption read, "*Enchantingly beautiful Catherine Leigh accepts the Best Actress Oscar in a full-length sequin-covered navy-blue gown and elegant diamond earrings.*"

"Yuck," gagged Molly, her mind swirling with the evidence that she had always been right about Leigh. She had figured it out long ago why that woman was in Kyle's life. It was so clear. This bitch was using him to gain notoriety, fame, and fortune. Leigh didn't love Kyle. She was too much into herself.

There was another picture of Leigh laughing with Kyle. No, Molly surmised, she was laughing *at* him, and he was so honorable he couldn't see it.

Molly knew she needed to hurry and get back to work, but that stupid smiling face staring up at her required pressing action. Molly grabbed her purse and removed a windowed envelope full of small, cut-up pictures. With a glue stick, she painstakingly stuck her face over Leigh's on each page that held the images.

"Molly!"

It was the restaurant manager, Bradford.

"You have three tables complaining you haven't served them. One table just walked out. Get out there."

Molly looked up, mortified at being caught. "Sorry, give me a second to put up my things."

"No, I said *now*, Molly!" In frustration, Bradford grabbed the magazine from her hand, twisted it, and threw it in the greasy garbage container.

"I've put up with your peculiar behavior over these rags for years," he thundered. "No more!"

"No!" she screeched and ran over to the garbage, frenziedly retrieving the magazine. She carefully wiped it off and slowly smoothed it out, gazing smitten at the picture of Kyle. "I'm so sorry, Kyle."

Bradford scowled, both shocked and furious at the same time. The other waitress entered, trying to stay out of the way.

"Molly, I've had it. Clean out your locker. You're fired!"

He turned to walk away, but Molly charged to him, gripping his arm.

"No, please. I need this job."

Bradford yanked his arm from her grasp. "No, you're fired. Get out." He looked at the other waitress. "Libby, you take Molly's section too … I'll help." Bradford led Libby back out to the dining room.

Molly clutched the magazine to her chest and glanced down, seeing her glued face had fallen off a picture of Leigh. Pungent hatred swelled within. It was all *her* fault … Catherine Leigh. That slut was mocking her, provoking her, keeping her away from the man she loved … the man who loved only Molly.

Molly tilted back on her open locker, oblivious to the chaos of the kitchen, staring at the open magazine, lost in a sea of muddled fantasy. She reflected on how she and Bret had gone to the movies to see Kyle. And when they made love, Bret had been so gentle … so tender … yes, it was Kyle in her bed, wasn't it? "Don't give up on me," she could still hear Bret … no, Kyle, whisper.

She tried to focus, fighting the confusion.

"Kyle's eyes," she said in a faint voice, analyzing his photo. "So blue, so loving."

Molly shook her head violently, her anger searing. "Evil bitch," she grumbled. "Touching my Kyle."

Molly took her belongings and slammed the locker, igniting a spark of clarity. She had to save her man from this spider who had lured him into her web.

Suddenly, Molly saw her enraged ex-boss stomping toward her. She was deaf to him. His lips were moving ferociously, but the sound was muffled. The only thing she distinctly heard was her mother's cruel cackle … or was it the spew from Leigh's ugly lips?

Chapter 20
Winning and Losing

*S*tudying the mantel, Cate was enveloped by a delicious sense of satisfaction, her Oscar next to Kyle's. It was fitting. And to be here at the ranch, the one place steeped in tranquility and love.

"Mom, Dad wants to know if we should grill some steaks tonight?" Robbie shut the door behind him to keep out the crisp air.

What a delightfully common question, she reflected. "Sounds yummy."

"It looks cool, Mom … you and Dad both have Oscars. You did good, Mom."

Cate put her arm about Robbie's shoulder, pulling him to her. He was presently a couple of inches taller than her, and Scott, every bit of sixteen years of age, towered over her. Her little boys were turning into young men.

She put on her jacket and went outside with Robbie. Mia was chasing Oakley and giggling her cares away. Scott was sitting with Kyle at the outdoor table with a fire crackling in the pit, texting his friends.

"Yes to grilling, Dad," Robbie called, strolling toward the table.

"What were you two doing in there?" Kyle stoked the fire.

"I was admiring Mom's Oscar."

"Your mom gave an amazing performance," Kyle boasted.

"Yeah, we know," Robbie said as an aside.

Cate looked from Scott to Robbie. "What do you mean *you* know? You know because I won the Oscar?"

"No," Scott answered, "we saw it."

"No, no, no, no, no, you're too young to see that movie." Cate collapsed into a chair. "How did you see it?"

"Simple," Scott replied, setting his phone down. "Rob and I walked into the theater, bought two PG tickets, and *accidentally* entered the R-rated movie. Guess what, there you both were on the big screen." Robbie and Scott shared a look of mischievous camaraderie.

Cate put her hand on her forehead and glared at her husband. "Kyle, did you know they did that?"

"I guess … sort of," Kyle laughed. "Boys, notice what a lovely shade of red your mother's face has turned." Kyle squelched his amusement.

"Mom, you were good," Robbie began. "It was messed up when it looked like you were crazy and might have multiple personalities. You were really convincing."

Mia yelled for her brothers to help build a snowman, although there was little snow left on the ground. Both Robbie and Scott rose to go out to her.

Scott waited for an instant and added, "Mom, don't worry. Dad told us you used a body double during the love scene. It's nice knowing it wasn't actually you."

While the kids played, Kyle switched chairs and sat next to Cate. He picked up her hand and kissed it.

"You okay?" he asked sympathetically.

Cate rested her head on his shoulder. "It wasn't a body double," she sighed.

"They never need to know," Kyle said in a soft voice. "But I do."

The middle of March can be gloomy on the coast. The sky was cloudy and dull, the ocean waves crashing thunderously on the shore.

Closing the door, Kyle walked onto the deck with a large blanket in his arms and wrapped it over Cate's shoulders.

"Honey, it's freezing out here. Why don't you come in where it's warm?"

Cate held his hands on her shoulders, and he sat in a chair behind her.

"It's such a strange feeling, Kyle. Like I'm an orphan. First, Aunt Mary, and now Mom. It's too much loss ..." She covered her eyes with her hands. Kyle moved his chair beside her.

"Honey, I know. I felt the same way after Nana died." He peeled her hands from her face and gazed at her, "Thank God I had you." He stroked her head. "I'm here, Catie. Whatever you need."

"Kyle, I loved my mother." Her look sought relief.

"I know, sweetheart. Cate, your mom loved you too, and she was a part of your life. She was at our wedding; she adored her grandchildren. My goodness, she attended every one of your performances of *Mamma Mia!*"

Shivering from the cold, Cate tugged the blanket up to her nose and slumped down, resembling a turtle in its shell.

"She watched you win an Oscar," Kyle consoled. "I never saw a mother prouder of her daughter. You both were happy together."

Cate lowered the blanket from her mouth to speak clearly. "It wasn't her fault."

Kyle adjusted the blanket to better cover his wife. "What wasn't her fault?"

"Those difficult times she and I had. I never told her what I needed from a mother."

"You never told anyone what you needed," he smiled.

Seeing Cate shiver, Kyle rapidly rubbed the blanket along her arms. "You're freezing. Please, let's go inside." He helped her up, Cate pressing herself close to him for body heat.

Placing his hand on the door handle, Kyle halted.

"I better warn you," he alerted, "Robbie's upset. He demands you explain why Emily gets Grandma's convertible Corvette, and he gets Grandpa's framed military flag. He says he never met Grandpa."

Cate exhaled, reminded of the everyday life scenario she so deeply wanted.

"Because he's fourteen, and we're buying him the car he's already picked out for his sixteenth birthday. Besides, Emily was her grandchild too."

"Exactly," Kyle nodded. "But you do know logic is not one of Robbie's best attributes right now?"

The warmth inside their home was inviting, swaddling them in coziness. Before Cate could flee to the bedroom, Robbie confronted his mother.

"Mom, it's totally unfair Emily gets Grandma's convertible. Grandma always told me I was her favorite. She'd want me to have it."

Cate glanced at Kyle. He shrugged with a perceptive smile. At once, the absurdity of it all struck Cate, and she burst our laughing. Cate's reaction tickled Kyle, who struggled to suppress joining her. Robbie stood there, confused and indignant.

"Thanks, Mom," Cate said, looking up to the heavens, while rubbing her neck. "Oh, Robbie, we're not laughing at you, sweetie. It's Grandma's final joke."

Robbie marched off to his room. Kyle embraced Cate, cherishing their parental trials.

Chapter 21
Blink of an Eye

The fundraiser was Hollywood sophistication at its finest. Cate and Kyle joined Edward and Beverly on the museum's main floor area, altered into a bar and entertainment space. Music and drink enticed participants to loosen their purse strings and give generously to the arts and various charities. The gathering was packed with fashionably dressed, famous, and influential attendees. Cate was dressed in a stunning off-the-shoulder, form-fitting champagne-colored gown with a side slit, and Kyle looked dashing in a custom-tailored black tuxedo. Edward and Beverly were formally dressed but in a more modest sense of elegance.

Beverly checked out the room, more accustomed to corporate power brokers than the glittery Hollywood elite.

"Cate, look at you," said Beverly. "Every bit the movie star."

"Not quite over the top like some people around here," Edward grinned.

Beverly laughed. "Edward's right, Cate. At least you don't have jewels dripping all over your body."

Edward sniffed the air. "My, my, the distinct aroma of money."

"And fame," Cate chuckled.

Kyle glanced at the oversized art deco clock on the wall. It read 8:45. "Our dinner seating is in an hour. We need to make the rounds and check out the auction items before finding our table."

"It's so crowded in here," Edward noted, trying out the hors d'oeuvres. "How do you expect to find anyone?"

"C'mon, Ed," Cate elbowed. "Kyle knows how to work a room

almost as well as you do."

After roaming around for about an hour, greeting different industry acquaintances, it was time to work their way upstairs for the late dinner.

Edward weaved his way through the crowd to find Cate and Kyle.

"I'll get Beverly." Edward took out his phone. "Hey, Bev, where are you? We're going upstairs to be seated for dinner."

Not wanting to scream over the chatter, Cate spoke close to Kyle's ear. "I need to make a stop at the powder room first. Something's in my eye, and it's starting to hurt. Back in a minute."

She gave him a quick kiss.

The restroom appeared to be empty. Standing at the mirror, Cate rummaged through her purse for eye drops to dislodge whatever flicked in her eye. Having some relief from the drops, she washed her hands. The door opened and a staff member entered, standing directly behind her. Cate glanced up. The woman seemed vaguely familiar.

"Hello," Cate weighed guardedly.

"Do you actually believe he loves you?"

Thoughts flashed through Cate's awareness. Why the hostile stance? Why is this woman so angry? Does she think I'm someone else?

"Excuse me?" Cate studied the woman's image in the mirror.

"He doesn't. He has always loved me."

Cate unquestionably recognized the voice. Turning slowly to face her, Cate asked, "Who do you mean?"

"My love, of course, Kyle. He's mine!" The woman removed a shiny .38 special from her uniform's pocket and aimed it at Cate's stomach.

The stranger on the beach ... Cate's mind withdrew ... a rushing panic taking charge, turning sharply to slow-motion images of her children ... a three-year-old Robbie ... Mia's first step, which she took to Robbie ... a seriously ill Scott clutching her hand in the hospital ... Oakley jumping on Kyle ... Kyle ... his touch ... his gaze...

A restroom stall door slowly opened, catching Cate's notice, and slapping her back into the present. A socialite slinked out, pressing herself against the wall. Terrified, she gradually made her way to the door. The woman from the beach glimpsed at the socialite's reflection in the mirror but stayed fixed on Cate.

"Seven years you've had him under some sort of spell," the woman spat, leveling the gun at Cate's heart. "I'm taking him back."

Kyle, Edward, and Beverly stood in the congestion near the staircase, waiting for Cate to return from the restroom.

Suddenly, a man's voice bellowing over the band's sound system repeatedly ordered everyone to immediately clear the area. Through the vast, windowed walls, police cars could be seen surrounding the building.

Kyle was confused, tense, trying to make sense of the chaos. His mind flashed on Cate ... not the time for her to be in the restroom.

"What's going on?" Edward questioned a security guard holding back the group.

"Not at liberty to say, sir," he responded in a forbidding tone. "Please stay back for your safety."

Kyle craned his neck to shift through the crowd, overhearing pieces of blurred chatter ... "Oscar winner ... Catherine Leigh ... gun ..."

"Cate!" Kyle yelled, shoving the huddled guests aside to get to the line of police now barricading part of the central area leading to the restroom hallway. Edward was right behind him. Two police officers blocked them. Kyle pushed forward, shouting, "I think my wife's in there!"

Cate felt as if she was watching her own fear and disorientation, Kyle and the children at the borders of her consciousness. She tried frantically to remain lucid, forcing down the suffocating feeling of numbness overtaking her.

"You were on the beach," she managed to say, her mouth dry and shaken. "Who are you?"

"You know who I am. You've stopped all my letters. You've kept Kyle from finding me." Molly brandished the gun in Cate's face. "I'm

96

Molly Lambert … I'm the love of Kyle's life!"

"Molly, I'm sorry, I didn't … I don't know anything about …"

"Stop lying, you deceitful whore! My letters. Did you read my words before you destroyed them? Kyle doesn't know how much I love him, does he?" Molly's fury reignited. "Evil bitch … did you plot all this with my mother?"

"I don't know your mother, Molly. Please …"

"She's dead."

"I'm so sorry Molly, for your loss." Cate tried to humanize the situation. "My mother died too."

"You think it's bad she's dead? It's wonderful! She's out of my way." Molly gave a manic laugh. "You're next."

Eyeing the deadly gun, Cate could hear the noise outside the restroom door. Her heart was pounding violently.

"Molly, let's talk about this. What if we go to the main room? Kyle's waiting there for me. You could talk to him. Tell him how you feel. Plan your future together. Wouldn't *that* make you happy?"

"Yes, I should talk to him," Molly reasoned.

"Well, we need to go out there." The outside noise grew louder.

"Why?" Molly glared suspiciously at Cate.

"Well, Kyle can't come into the ladies' room. There's a comfortable sitting area where you can talk and get to know each other." Cate's intellect was working, figuring. She needed to get Molly out of the restroom.

"Kyle and I already know each other," Molly sneered. "You'll only get in the way."

"No, I won't. I swear. You can have a long conversation."

"And you'll tell Kyle the truth," Molly panted. "You'll tell him what you've done and that you never loved him."

There was something about Molly's words—*you never loved him*—that, despite the raging horror, gave Cate a pissed-off edge of strength. She would never say those words. No one would tell her how to die.

"So, let's go see Kyle." Cate ever so gradually crept toward the door, the gun following her every movement.

"No," Molly blurted, darkness dimming her mood. "You have to be dead first."

The restroom door opened, and Cate walked out very slowly with her hands up, shaking with terror.

Kyle and Edward broke through to the other side of the security barrier, strangers prying into their world from all areas. Cate spotted the strobing blue lights outside the windows and felt the presence of police everywhere even though she couldn't see them through her tears. Her sensory perceptions were intensified, though. She could hear every squeak of a shoe on the hard floor and every cough, and she heard Edward cry out when he saw her, "Dear God!" Her sight locked on Kyle, filled with fright and regret.

"Stop," Molly demanded. Cate stiffened. "Turn around. Don't you dare look at him!"

Cate rotated, keenly aware she was still fighting panic, Molly's gun now pressed against her chest.

Kyle and Edward overheard the communication from the police officer's earpiece. The SWAT team couldn't risk taking a shot with Molly holding the gun against Cate's body.

Please, God, this can't be happening, Kyle's brain cried, dread surging through him. He had to do something. Guilt showered him, blaming himself for not taking the threat seriously years ago … and he promised Cate he'd never let anything hurt her. On instinct, Kyle wrestled past the police officer's arm, breaking the detention, and rushed towards Cate.

Cate anxiously turned, her wits screaming within her mind, "No, Kyle, stay back."

"I told you not to look at him," Molly furiously exclaimed, pushing the gun harder against Cate's heart.

"Molly. Hey!" Kyle drew Molly's focus to him. As it was difficult to miss, he saw straightaway that Molly was trying to look exactly like Cate … hair dyed auburn and styled identically to hers, made up to mimic Cate in every way.

"Kyle, my love," she swooned. "I knew you wouldn't forget."

"Forget?" Kyle responded, the actor within him staring deep into her eyes, enticing her to keep her interest on him. "No. I remember you."

"Of course, I'm your true love, Kyle. Not her." Molly was enraptured. "Tell me, sweetheart, how much you love me and that we'll always be together." Molly aggressively aimed at Cate. "She's evil. She's jealous of our happiness. She tried to stop our love, burning all my love letters to you."

Molly slightly repositioned herself and Cate to face Kyle better. "I'm going to kill her … for us."

"Don't do that, Molly," Kyle caringly pleaded, still trusting his acting skills. "You're not someone who would do that sort of thing. You're good and kind."

"Oh, Kyle, you don't know all she's done to us," Molly cried. "Come closer. You need to hear the truth from this bitch."

Molly painfully shoved the gun deeper into Cate's chest, the cold tip of the weapon bruising Cate's skin. "Tell him what you told me. Tell him you never …"

Cate's hands, held up in the air, were trembling uncontrollably. Her engagement and wedding rings caught the light of the room and flashed into Molly's eyes.

"Take those off," Molly commanded, her purpose jumbled by the glow. "They don't belong to you. They're mine! Put them on my finger, now!" Keeping the gun steady, Molly raised her left hand, wiggling her ring finger in Cate's face.

Cate worked off the two rings with her hands still overhead, humiliation and anger mixing with fear.

"May I lower my hands?" Cate asked.

"Yes," Molly gushed, her right hand sliding the gun from Cate's chest to her stomach.

Shaking, Cate placed the engagement ring on Molly's finger.

"You have small fingers," Molly commented. "I'll need to get them resized." She held her hand under Cate's nose, flaunting the large diamond on the engagement ring. "How big is it?"

"Four and a half carats," Kyle answered within a few feet of them.

Molly was mesmerized by the ring on her finger, captured by the diamond's sparkle.

Kyle stole a loving gaze at Cate, their eyes momentarily connecting. "Flawless," he said with penetrating tenderness in his voice.

"Yes, flawless," Molly agreed, still looking at the ring. Kyle and Cate's eyes darted back to Molly. "Like our love, darling." Molly abruptly looked up to Kyle, then turned back to Cate. "Put the wedding ring on me," she demanded.

Tears streaming down her cheeks, Cate hovered the ring over Molly's finger but fumbled the exchange, the ring falling to the top of Molly's foot.

"Idiot," Molly scowled, awkwardly bending over to pick up the ring, momentarily pulling the gun from Cate's stomach. Without faltering, Kyle charged forward to Cate, tackling her to the ground ... two shots fired.

Protectively covered by Kyle, Cate lay on the marble floor, her skull aching from the crash. Disoriented, she saw Molly's lifeless body, eyes wide open with a vacant stare.

"Kyle," Cate cried, trying to sense if she had been shot. She didn't feel a bullet. There was no pain ... except her head ... so dazed ... there was wetness. She lifted her hand to see it covered with blood. Again, the world turned in slow motion.

"Kyle," she repeated. No response, his weight heavy on her. "Kyle? Oh, my God, somebody help him! Help!"

Cate felt a rush of people surrounding her. Hands gently picked him up and pulled her away. She tried to move, but other strange arms held her down. "Just relax, breathe," someone said.

Out of the blue, there was Edward. She tried to rise, collapsing in his arms.

It was two a.m., and the emergency room was a madhouse. Cate couldn't function emotionally or physically, her head throbbing in pain, leaving Edward to fill out paperwork and speak to the doctors.

Two police officers entered and approached Cate, sitting in the waiting room with Beverly.

"Ms. Leigh?" the first officer called to her.

Edward intercepted the officers. "It's Mrs. Weston, and how can I help you? I'm her attorney."

Edward consulted with the officers, shielding Cate from a painful interrogation. At the end of the debriefing, one of the officers handed

Cate's engagement and wedding rings to Edward.

"Thank you for your cooperation, Mr. Leigh. And give Mrs. Weston our best."

"I will, thank you." Edward shuffled Cate's rings in his hand and placed them in his pocket. He would give them to her when she was more stable.

Julia entered with a bag in her hand, listening to the end of the conversation. She smiled at Edward. "Cate always said it was great to have a lawyer in the family. Can you do something to disperse the crowd outside? It's insane out there. Getting in here was nearly impossible."

"Vultures," Edward grumbled, shaking his head.

"How's Cate?" Julia touched Edward's arm.

Edward was exhausted in his concern. "Physically? I don't know. She's still in shock. They want to run a CAT scan and treat her injuries. She won't go until she has word on Kyle. Emotionally? See for yourself."

Julia was shaken by how fragile Cate appeared, still dressed in her party attire, covered in Kyle's blood. Cate examined her hands, lost in the simplest of actions, often kneading her naked ring finger and rubbing her palms together as if they were still covered with blood and she was trying to wipe them clean. Cate's mind was erratic and confused, incessantly replaying the horror … the falling ring … Kyle diving … gunshots … Molly's eyes … Kyle's blood.

"Cate." Julia sat down and held her hand. "How is he?"

Cate brought her awareness to Julia.

"I … I have no idea. They took Kyle away to treat him. He never regained consciousness." Cate was traumatized. Mascara streaked down her cheeks from crying. "It's my fault. All she wanted was for me to say I didn't love him. I couldn't, even if it was a lie. I couldn't do it. I expected to die. It should be me, not Kyle."

"No, it shouldn't be either of you. It's not your fault." Julia held her. "She wasn't sane."

"My children?" Cate wailed in panic. "I need to see my children. Where are they?"

"I called Emily. She's with the boys and Mia," Edward reassured. "The police are stationed outside your house and said they will bring them to the hospital first thing in the morning."

Julia stood up and gently tugged Cate's arm. "Let's get you cleaned up. Mia can't see you like this. It'll frighten her. I brought some of my clothes for you. Come on, let's go to the restroom to get you changed."

"I don't think I'll ever feel safe in a restroom again."

"You'll have me there. We're safe now."

Flashes went off from outside the window, following Cate and Julia from the room.

"They're such cockroaches," Beverly stood and walked over to Edward. "They're the real villains." She put her arm around Edward's waist. "You know when everything happened at the museum, and you were kneeling over to hold Cate? I heard a tabloid jerk make a snide comment that Cate was already replacing her husband. I wanted to smack him. I did yell at him, 'He's her brother, you human slime.' Half the museum heard me."

Edward glared at the paparazzi lurking at the window.

"Damn it! We need privacy," Edward snarled.

There, standing before the mirrors in her underwear with blood coating her skin, Cate's legs went weak, and she had to sit on the floor. With wet paper towels, Julia helped Cate wash off the blood which had seeped through her dress. Julia was a good mother, and that was precisely what Cate needed … a mother.

She gave Cate a pair of slacks, a blouse, and a sweater to keep the hospital's coolness at bay.

"You helped me with my wedding dress, Julia," Cate spoke almost childlike.

Julia had no response that wasn't heartbreaking.

"There. You look better." Julia could see dried blood in Cate's hair. "Now we're going to get you checked out. A head injury is nothing to take lightly."

Cate peeked up with sincere gratitude. "Thank you, Julia. Thank you for being my friend."

Julia hugged her. "You're more than my friend. You're like a sister."

Holding Cate's hand, the way a mother would hold her child's hand, Julia led her to the exam rooms.

The children entered the waiting room at dawn's first light, the boys having not slept, restless with worry. Guaranteeing the kids weren't harassed by the press and paparazzi upon entering had been a logistical nightmare for Edward. When everyone settled down, the doctor came out to speak to Cate. She stepped away, motioning for Edward to follow her. Cate clung to her brother.

"Mrs. Weston, it was a difficult surgery," Dr. Richardson stated. "He has lost a significant amount of blood. I assessed whether any vital organs were damaged. As far as we can tell, they haven't been compromised. The bullet is still lodged inside in a challenging position. We're bringing in a specialist skilled at these types of surgeries, and Mr. Weston stands the best chance of a positive recovery."

"Doctor, will he … is he … going to be okay?" Cate could barely speak, not asking the question haunting her … *will he live?*

"He's stable for now. Be patient, and if you pray, do so." Dr. Richardson left, his lingering words slaughtering hope.

Cate lowered herself to a seat, her face marred with excruciating agony.

Mia climbed onto Cate's lap and cuddled against her mother's chest, still quite sleepy. Robbie sat on one side of his mom, and she held his hand. Scott sat down on the other side of Cate and put his arm on the back of her chair.

Cate stared at the floor. She was mute, drowned in smothering emotions. All her resilience had been drained from her like the blood that covered her hands and dress.

Chapter 22
Gathering Storm

By mid-morning, police had controlled access to the waiting room, still working to disperse the large crowd of fans and paparazzi outside the windows and into the parking lot. The Weston family was given a secluded location to wait for word from the specialist who came in for the surgery.

Tom Jenkins was allowed entry at noon, bringing the family much-appreciated relief from hospital cafeteria food.

He tried to find a delicate and subtle way to introduce the subject. "Cate, the limited series shoot next week? They can't push the filming back for you."

"I know. I won't leave Kyle. I need to be here." Cate sought his empathy. "Tom, I'm so weary. I want to take my family and hide from the world."

"Of course, I understand," he reassured, holding her hand. "There'll be other projects."

Cate looked away bleakly, not hearing much of what was being said.

"Be strong." He said as he left, taking with him a project she had once believed she honestly had to have … a perfect chance for an Emmy. All she wanted now was Kyle. All she *ever* really wanted was Kyle.

Although Mia had not yet turned five, she tried to be patient because Daddy was hurt. Her brothers and Emily kept her entertained through the long day. The hours drifted into the evening with no word, and Mia grew more antsy and overtired.

Cate rocked Mia on her lap and murmured, "Aren't you getting sleepy?"

Mia nodded. Julia sat down beside Cate, rubbing her back for comfort.

"John and I are going to get some rest," she said quietly. "We'll be back in the morning. Would you like us to take Mia? We'd be happy to keep her with us until things settle down. And the boys as well."

"Julia, thank you. That's so kind of you."

"Mia, baby," Cate whispered to the nearly asleep child. "Aunt Julia and Uncle John would like to bring you home with them, and you can get some sleep. When Daddy's feeling better, you can visit him."

"I want to see Daddy now, Mommy," she whined, resisting sleep.

"Oh, baby, he's with the doctor. And he may be with the doctor for a while. Get some sleep, and you can visit him later." Cate turned to Scott and Robbie, "Boys, do you want to go too?"

"No, Mom," Robbie mumbled. Scott shook his head.

Mia was so tired she couldn't stand. Scott carried her, Mia laying her head on her brother's shoulder, falling asleep. He followed Julia and John, turning before he was out the door, and he mouthed to Cate, "I'll be right back."

Robbie hugged his mom. "It'll be fine, Mom."

Holding his hand, Cate reverted to her numb state. It would be another long night.

Cate rested between Scott and Robbie. It was almost four in the morning, and their room was dim, the light from the television casting a misty glow. Robbie had fallen asleep up against his mother's arm and shoulder. Scott had stretched out along the chairs with his head next to her leg, making a pillow of his jacket. Cate stroked Scott's hair while he slept.

In a near hypnotic state, Cate's blank stare drifted. She had repeatedly played softly on her phone John Hiatt's song, *Have a Little Faith in Me*. The music transported Cate back to 2008, alone and devastated by Alex's betrayal. Kyle could always sense her pain and traveled two thousand miles to be by her side in Florida.

The memory lulled her into a dream ...

It was dark, Cate's mind confused, panicked. Where was she? Where was Kyle?

"I'm here," came a sound from somewhere within the void. And then she saw him. Rushing to throw her arms around him, never had her embrace been tighter, feeling his heart beat against hers. She vowed not to let him go.

"Catie, I'm always with you," he whispered. "We're one."

Edward turned off the music, Cate startled from her restless dream. He watched his sister with concern as the surgeon entered.

"Mrs. Weston?"

"Yes," Cate called, jumping up and grabbing both of her sons' hands. Edward stood behind them with his hand on her shoulder.

"The surgery's over. Fortunately, the bullet missed the vital organs, but there was still significant internal bleeding from peripheral damage. We're extremely cautious about infections. There are also immediate issues. Mr. Weston's lost a great deal of blood and could remain unconscious for a while."

"A coma?"

"It's called hypovolemic shock. Once his levels have stabilized, he should regain consciousness. There's another more urgent issue. The bullet grazed the spinal cord. There is some paralysis. We won't know the extent for a while. It may or may not be permanent. Only time will tell. And I must tell you, pulmonary complications due to paralysis can be life-threatening. For now, he's stable. Tomorrow's unknown and these next few days are critical."

"When can we see him?" asked Edward.

"He's in recovery. I'm sorry, not everyone can visit. You may, Mrs. Weston. The nurse will be out in a few minutes to take you back."

Cate slowly lowered herself to the seat to absorb what she had heard, the doctor's words hanging in the air like a thick fog. Tears welled in her eyes, chin quivering.

Cate's attention drew to the television screen as Edward picked up the remote and turned up the volume.

"Kyle Weston remains in critical condition after attempting to protect his wife, actress Catherine Leigh, who was being held at gunpoint by an assailant identified as Molly Lambert. Lambert was fatally shot at the scene by the LAPD. Both Weston and Leigh are Academy Award-winning actors, Ms. Leigh winning her award this past February. We will keep you updated on Kyle Weston's condition."

Cate glanced away, quiet words leaking from her lips. "I can't …"

"You can't what, honey?" Edward put his hands on top of hers.

"I don't want any of it, the Oscar, my career. I only want Kyle." The fear crushed her. "Ed, he has to be okay. I can't do this without him."

"We're ready." The nurse's presence startled everyone.

Edward helped Cate up, staring into her weeping eyes. "It's going to be okay, Sis, I promise."

Cate suffered a labored breath and followed the nurse, winding through dull inner hallways toward Kyle's room.

The door opened, Cate entering a warped, unrecognizable world. Her eyes probed the room, her heart rapidly pounding. It was a scene from her own personal horror film; the various machines clicking, whirring noises, lights and graphs, IVs hanging everywhere, tubes and oxygen hoses. Kyle was fixed within an apparatus encompassing his entire body. Cate examined the device as it rotated the bed from facing downward to upright. This was the most intimidating contraption she had ever seen. It was as if the man she loved had been swallowed by technology. Cate was petrified.

"Kyle, please wake up," she begged, slipping her hand beneath his.

Cate felt herself lessening. Here before her was the meaning of love, the man she treasured, her best friend and soulmate. She could barely breathe. The grief that he may slip away from her … she demanded his return … and yet had no power.

It should have been me, she thought. I should be lying here, not you.

"Kyle, we'll get through this together," she said softly, hoping he might hear. "And we'll be stronger for it. I love you, Kyle Weston. Never forget, I can't live without you. Sweetheart, you can't leave me."

She gently kissed him, waiting as she prayed for a response.

"I love you," she vowed.

As she left the recovery room to return to her family, Cate asked the nurse, "What's that thing he's in?"

"It's to readjust his positioning for blood flow, Mrs. Weston. There's a risk an embolism might form from a lack of movement due to paralysis. We'll monitor him constantly."

Once again, Cate's heart sank.

Chapter 23
Secret Life

Two weeks had gone by with Kyle coming in and out of consciousness. Despite grim reports concerning the speed of improvement, Cate held on to a modicum of hope. Still, the suffocating guilt and longing tore her apart.

She was usually accompanied to the hospital by her security guard, George Vernan. A former police officer with honorable service in the military, he was in his mid-forties with a commanding presence and no immediate family to distract him. A perfect fit for the role, George was sharp and hawkish in his watch.

The children also had security. For Mia, there was the bubbling and charismatic Lynn Revers. Only 28 years old, she was a highly trained security expert who the kids assumed was Mia's nanny. Lynn's presence was playful and stable for both Mia and her worried mother.

Although the children were perpetually guarded, Cate would often excuse George for the day. His watchful care often invaded Cate's need for privacy, making her crave solitude.

Cate sat silently at Kyle's bedside, hoping her focus on him might chase away the distress and blame. Edward entered the room and looked around the area.

"Catherine, where's George?"

She gazed at Kyle. "I gave him the day off."

"Catherine, you can't keep doing that. Come with me. I have to talk to you."

Sluggishly, not having any desire to move, she dragged herself after her brother to the unoccupied waiting room and took a seat.

"I need to show you this report." Sitting beside her, Edward opened a thick folder.

"On what?" Cate stared at the doorway to Kyle's room.

"Molly Lambert."

"I don't want to hear about her. It doesn't matter." Cate jumped up and started toward the door. Edward grabbed her arm, pulling her back to the seats.

"Yes, it does. Look at this. My investigators were given access to what the police found when they closed the case on her."

"Ed, I don't ..." She put up her hand defiantly.

"Listen," he hissed.

Cate peered at the floor.

"They interviewed her old apartment manager. He evicted her right before ..." Edward chose his words carefully, "the incident. She didn't return to her place to be served the notice, though. So, she never cleared out her things. Here are pictures of the interior of her apartment."

Edward moved the file of photos in front of her. One whole wall was littered with tabloid covers and article photos of Kyle. There were also pictures of Molly's cut-out face over Cate's. On others, Molly had blanked out Cate's face and scribbled *Slut!* and *Whore!* over her body. Next to Kyle's photos, she had written *My Man*, and *I love Molly*.

Edward handed her a picture of an elaborately decorated box, Kyle's name written across it. "Inside, there were more than a dozen love letters addressed to Kyle, sealed and ready to be sent," he said. "A part of her must have believed she had mailed them like the ones she sent him back in 2012."

"Why are you showing me this?" Cate glared at her brother in disgust.

"It wasn't your fault. She wasn't stable. You were standing in her way. She had to get rid of her competition." Edward took a deep breath. "And you weren't the only one at risk."

He turned to the last picture. The cover photo of Kyle with Cate and

Mia, their daughter's face aggressively scratched out, and an X drawn over her body with the words *NOT KYLE'S*.

"We talked to a neighbor who said she was terrified of dogs. Put it together, Catherine. Oakley saved you … and Mia. Lambert might have killed you both on the beach that day if your dog hadn't reacted as he did."

Suddenly, a new level of terror consumed Cate, replaying the strange woman on the beach, Molly's hand fiddling with something in her right pocket.

"Why are you telling me all this? She's dead." Cate started to rise, wanting to break free from the images playing in her head, but Edward pulled her back to a seated position.

"Do you think she's the only one out there?" Edward placed the folder in her lap again. "Catherine, you can't keep sending George home because you don't like being followed. You need security."

"What I need is peace and quiet." Cate shoved the folder back to Edward.

"You're both celebrities. Next time it could be someone who goes after Kyle because of being obsessed with you." Cate felt stung by Edward's reproach but knew he was right.

"The only problem I have is a vindictive ex-husband," she said with a tone of resentment.

"What do you mean?" Edward set down the folder in the empty seat next to him.

"The tabloids. They're running tell-all stories about Kyle and me before I was divorced. They're salacious lies based on tales Alex is spinning for them. I'm sure he's enjoying the spotlight of being the poor, cockled spouse. I wonder how much they're paying him to attack my critically wounded husband." Tears streaked down her cheeks again. "His timing is inexcusably ugly!"

"Want me to stop it?" Edward took her hand.

"It doesn't matter. None of it matters," she sobbed, "I just want my friend back. I want Kyle."

Edward reached over to hold her, his mind flooding with anger.

Chapter 24
Howling at the Moon

*E*very morning after the kids left for school, Cate went to the hospital. In the beginning, Edward and Julia kept Cate company. Soon Edward had to get back to work and Julia back to her life with John. Only Cate remained vigil at Kyle's bedside from dawn to dusk—often forgetting to eat and never truly resting.

Kyle's progress was painfully slow, each day an unknown. One day he'd be improving, the next regressing. Most days, he'd fluctuate between unconsciousness and incoherence, Cate unable to communicate with him, both frustrating and frightening. She'd convinced herself she saw signs of improvement … and then a doctor would bring the reality check.

Another week went by.

Cate was weak from a lack of sleep and nourishment, her unstable emotions under relentless attack.

The children were at school, Edward was in New York for a week's worth of depositions, and Julia traveled with John to Minneapolis on business. Having again given George the day off, Cate was alone with no support when she went to the hospital that morning.

The staff dashed feverishly.

"Mrs. Weston!" Kyle's attending physician hurriedly approached, blocking her from entering his room.

"I'm sorry, Mrs. Weston, we have an emergency here," said Dr.

Trask, his voice commanding. "We're moving your husband to critical care."

Cate's stomach sank. "What's wrong?" Her body trembled beyond control.

"Mr. Weston's condition has deteriorated. His body's fighting an infection. He has septicemia and is sepsis. It's common but quite serious with his type of wound. We're giving him high doses of antibiotics."

Now, she was panic-stricken—this could not be happening!

"Can I see him?" Cate's consciousness seemed to be outside her body, watching her speak.

"I'm afraid not. You can't stay. The next few hours are critical, and we will be actively monitoring your husband's care."

"Please, doctor. I'll stay out of the way."

"I'm sorry. Any exposure could be fatal. We'll call you with updates."

The doctor swiftly entered Kyle's room, closing the door behind him.

Cate wasn't aware of driving herself to Malibu. Somehow, she made it home without incident. Her mind scattered, she entered the beach house as if it were the first time and slowly turned in a circle, visually inspecting every corner and nook, hoping to discover something new and comforting ... a miracle perhaps.

Oakley followed Cate to the beach, his tail no longer wagging. The ocean was violent, deafening waves fueled by an unexpected storm. Numb and exhausted, Cate moved closer to the water's edge, entranced by the power of the swell ... her mind matching its fury. Cate's breathing turned shallow and fast, her pain becoming a force within itself, bursting out with uncontrollable anger. She screamed at the sea, the sky, the helplessness. Falling to her knees, she barely noticed the punishment of the surging tide. And still, she screamed.

Oakley crept up behind her, tail between his legs, body drenched, mind uncertain ... his instinct to protect her.

From his deck, Mark heard the wail and peered out. Quickly glancing to the sky to see if any helicopters were lurking, he whistled for Roxie and ran down his deck stairs toward Cate.

Within a few feet of Cate, Oakley wagging his tail at the familiar friend, Mark gently asked, "Cate, honey, are you okay?"

Cate shook her head and sobbed, fear shadowing her eyes. "He might not make it, Mark. I can't lose him. I can't."

"You won't. He's a fighter." Mark worriedly skimmed the area. "Cate, why don't we get you inside? Paparazzi are everywhere out here. Let's not give them a headline. Come on, let's get you home."

Cate reluctantly rose and wandered over to the stairs leading to her deck. Mark followed, surveying the region for paparazzi. Once he helped her to the deck stairs, he watched her climb up.

She stopped and glimpsed back. Mark waited at the bottom step. "Aren't you coming up?" she pleaded.

"I shouldn't. Prying eyes."

"Mark, you're a friend and neighbor."

"I know. Paparazzi."

"Right," Cate mumbled, fighting the sorrow. "The price for being who we are?"

"I'm sorry, kid." Solemnly he shook his head. "Cate, are you going to be all right?"

"I have to be." She sat down on the top step with Oakley beside her. "I'm forced to pretend I have it all together, and I don't. I can't control anything. I want to curl up and disappear."

"I can't imagine what you're going through."

"Thanks." Cate gave Mark an appreciative smile and entered the house with Oakley.

Mark began to walk away, taking his cell phone from his back pocket.

"Hi, my name is Mark Tylare. Is Edward Leigh available? It's an emergency ... Tell him it's about his sister ... I'm her neighbor ..."

"Mom!" Scott yelled out, rushing in the front door with Robbie.

Cate was asleep on the living room floor, resting on Oakley. The boys stood over the two of them.

"Boys," Cate sat up hastily, her mind cloudy. "What is it?"

Cate pushed back her hair. She was a mess from crying and covered in dried salt water and sand.

"Uncle Ed called," Scott announced. "He's flying home right now."

"Why? He's in depositions all week."

"Mom, why are you covered in sand?" Robbie raised.

"Oakley and I were walking in the surf." Cate stared between the two of them. "Why are you home early?"

"Uncle Ed talked to our schools and had us released today. Told us to get here right away." Scott crossed to the broom closet to get a dustpan and broom.

"What's the big emergency?" Cate snuggled Oakley.

"Mom, please stop," Scott said, acting mature.

"Stop what?"

"Believing you must do this on your own and keep the truth from us. Rob and I are old enough to know what's going on. We're a family, and we're stronger together."

"You're not alone, Mom," Robbie added. "So, go shower before Lynn brings Mia home from school. We'll clean up."

"You might bathe Oakley too. He smells." Cate turned up her nose. "Boys, thank you. I love you both very much. I don't know what I'd do without you."

They both watched their mother, worry jamming their thoughts.

Kyle, secured in the contraption to rotate blood flow, was now surrounded by what resembled an oxygen tent. The enclosure's addition smacked of a bad sci-fi movie, making Cate, dressed in scrubs, feel powerless. The doctor had noted improvement, which allowed her to sit with him as long as she refrained from physical contact.

Cate fought the urge to crawl into Kyle's bed, so she could hold him and whisper all the things only he should hear from her lips. She also held back yet another flood of tears, revealing a brave face. So, if by a miracle he'd wake up, he'd see her courage and devotion, not her distress.

Cate stood to leave for the evening, still maintaining the pretense of strength. But, she thought, he did appear to be better.

"I love you, Kyle," she promised gently. "Always have, always will. See you tomorrow."

Cate left the room and changed out of her scrubs, shocked to see Edward waiting for her. "Ed!" She embraced him. "Ed, you're here."

Edward held his sister, calming her anguish.

"I talked to the doctor," he said, moving her at arm's length to meet her vision. "Kyle's turned a corner. He's getting stronger."

Cate's eyes filled with joy. A contented smile showed on both of their faces.

"Good news?" he grinned.

"Incredible news." Cate exhaled relief.

"Everything's going to be okay, honey."

"Ed, you came back from New York for me?" She wiped the tears from her cheek.

"Yes, of course. You're my sister." Edward took Cate's arm and walked down the corridor toward the hospital exit. "Mark Tylare called me and said he was worried about what happened on the beach this morning. So, what happened, Sis?"

Cate sighed, almost embarrassed. "I went for a walk and ended up yelling at the ocean … maybe it was the world. I've never done that before. I was convinced if I screamed loud enough, I'd get Kyle back." Cate glanced at her brother, concerned about his reaction.

"Mark heard me," she continued. "He probably thinks I'm crazy. Anyway, he was afraid someone would take a picture, and it would be on the cover of some rag. I guess I should say he didn't need to call you, that I'm fine. Ed, I'm so glad you're here."

Edward smiled compassionately.

"You're not crazy, Sis. You're allowed to howl at the moon."

Chapter 25
Uninvited Guest

C ate was loaded down with grocery bags when Scott rushed to her.

"Hey, sweetie," she said excitedly. "Mia napping? Thanks for babysitting."

Scott started to speak, but Cate kept talking. "Your dad's doing so much better! The infection's under control. He's awake, talking, and asking to see each of you. I know there's work to be done, but it's going to be fine. We'll visit him after dinner."

"Oh my gosh," said Scott, his eyes beginning to well. "That's such good news!"

Scott wiped his eyes, his look turning serious. "Mom, there's ..."

"I'm making your favorite tonight, Italian stew," she continued. "Uncle Ed will be here any minute with some papers for me to sign." Cate shelved the can goods in the pantry. "I told him what we were having for dinner. He'll stay. Uncle Ed loves to eat."

"Mom ..."

"Sorry, sweetie. You were saying something?"

"Yes, there's someone ..."

Before he could finish, Cate heard a greeting from the deck. "Hello, Catherine." She instantly felt sick.

She turned almost mechanically, breathing heavily. "Alex, what are you doing here? How did you get past security? Where's George?"

"Rob gave me the code and told your man to let me in."

Robbie came in off the deck, sensing he might have made a mistake. Scott clutched Cate's hand. "Mom, you need some help here in the kitchen?"

"Thank you, Scott," Cate answered, again realizing he had his father's intuitive and calming wisdom. Still, she never broke sight of Alex. "Will you and Robbie please bring in the rest of the groceries?"

"Come on, Rob."

"Alex, follow me out to the deck." Cate stomped outside and shut the double doors behind them. "So, what are you doing here?"

"I came to see my son."

"You're unreal." Cate tried to maintain her poise. "I offered to fly him to Alabama last week for a visit, and you were too busy to have anything to do with him. Now, for some reason, you jump on a plane and take a side trip to Malibu?"

"I wanted to check out where my son lives." Alex stretched over the railing. "This is a fancy place, Catherine. I can see why you dumped me and married the guy."

Cate stayed against the doors, out of the camera line of the open beach. "I've seen what you've been telling the gossip magazines. You certainly have rewritten history, haven't you?"

"Have I? What really happened with you and the famous Kyle Weston?"

"I never lied to you. I never betrayed our marriage. That was you, not me." She stood in a rebellious stance.

"All I know is the movie star whisked you away to this palace. He stole my family."

"No, he was helping out a friend." Cate detected how exposed they were to the potential of being photographed. "And you lost your family all on your own." She took a fiery breath. "Alex, why the unscheduled trip?"

"Just wanted to see how well you live. My life, not so great. You may not have heard, but it's been rough. I lost everything."

"I did, but the bankruptcy happened a few years ago, right? Adequate time, with hard work, to dig yourself out of a hole."

"It's not been easy. But you? Look at you. How swanky you are married to money. Was that your dream? Screwing your way to riches?"

"I won an Oscar. I make lots of money on my own, and my husband doesn't expect nor want me to support him, unlike our fiasco of a marriage."

"So, what do you do with all that cash you get for being famous?"

"I save it for my children. Isn't that what a good parent is supposed to do? Take care of their children? Of course, you wouldn't know, would you?" The disdain was rising, and she didn't care. "I *so* miss the old days before I married Kyle … my *ex*-husband weaseling out of his child support payments."

Alex laughed scornfully. "Well, this is pretty damn spectacular, Catherine."

Alex rashly moved forward, gripped her left hand, and leered at her wedding rings.

"Wow, some rock. Must have cost Kyle a week of work. I see why the tabloids made a big enough deal about this. *Flawless*? Must be referring to the ring, certainly not you."

"Let go," she seethed, yanking her hand away. "Do you enjoy kicking a man when he's fighting for his life?" She moved away from him. "What the hell do you want, Alex?"

Alex cornered her again, planting himself within a few inches of her face. "I just want to know … if he croaks … is this all yours?"

Cate slapped him hard.

"Hey," he blurted with a snarky grumble. "I could sue you for assault."

"You mean *battery*, and my brother would love to see you in court," she retaliated, walking toward the door. "Alex, my worst day with Kyle is a thousand times better than the best day with you ever was."

Alex scoffed, Cate returning to the living room. He promptly followed.

Although the boys could not hear the conversation, they had viewed Cate and Alex on the deck. It was obvious the discussion was not friendly. When Cate slapped Alex, Robbie instinctively jolted forward to intercede. Scott held him by the arm.

"If you're planning to protect one of your parents," Scott said, "it better be your mother."

Alex gave her a repulsed jeer. "I guess I'll get my son and leave." He motioned to Robbie, observing from the kitchen.

Scott continued to hold Robbie's arm. "Let's go to your bedroom and let them talk alone."

Mindful of the boys' presence, Cate stepped to the far side of the living room. Despite her rising irritation, she spoke with confidence. "No, he's *my* son. Stop using him like he's an ATM."

"What?"

"I know what you're doing. Robbie's not your do-over. You lived your life. Let him live his. He's not your pal. He's the child. You forgot that the day you decided to be a player instead of a responsible adult and a good father."

Everything in the room had shifted while she spoke. Cate sensed Robbie was now standing behind her and Scott standing behind him, listening to every word they were saying. Cate heard the front door open, then shut. Edward entered, halting to examine what was happening. Cate glanced at him and put her hand up to stop him from interceding.

"Catherine, those words are awfully familiar. I seem to recall Kyle saying them to me about you once. Let you live your life. And telling me to leave you alone. I'm sure it was only because he wanted to fuck you. Except you two had been doing that for a while, right?" He suggestively caressed her arm, and she pulled away. "You've been damaged goods since you were nineteen living here the first time. And to think I married trash … such a whore!"

A body lunged forward, bumping Cate back into a chair. Cate was shocked, witnessing Scott tussling to hold Robbie off Alex, who had lost his footing when Robbie shoved him away from his mom. Robbie looked rabid.

"Never talk to my mother like that ever again! You're a …" Robbie stifled his words. "I have parents. I don't need you. Get out!" Robbie withheld the tears within his rage, Scott leading him to his room, past his uncle, who gently squeezed Robbie's shoulder and nodded to Scott when they walked by. Cate stood shaking, with her hands covering her mouth.

"Well, he has your temper, doesn't he?" Alex stood up, brushing himself off.

"You heard Robbie. Get out of our home and never come back." Cate breathed heavily.

Alex straightened up and strutted out the door, not making eye contact with Edward.

"Alex," Edward yelled from behind, catching up with him near the gate.

"So, are you going to have a go at me now, ex-brother-in-law?"

"How much?"

"How much, what?" Alex abruptly stopped, spied George guarding the front gate, and turned to face Edward.

"How much to get you out of my sister's and Robbie's lives for good?" Edward went into his pocket and pulled out his cell phone.

"What makes you think I can be bought?"

"I'm in charge of Robbie's trust now. You aren't getting another dime from him. You have already drained eighty thousand dollars out of it. So, how much more to get rid of you forever?" Edward started typing notes on his phone, tactfully turning on the recorder.

"Half a million," Alex snipped as if it was a joke.

"Are you kidding? Damn, you have a high opinion of yourself," Edward mocked. "Two hundred and fifty thousand."

Alex pulled back his head. "Hardly a suitable offer," he responded, emboldened by his presumed negotiating skills. "After all, I have to pay back Rob ... or do I?"

"You're unbelievable. Two hundred and fifty thousand, and you can forget your eighty-thousand-dollar debt. I'll give it to my nephew. My final offer with one provision. A nondisclosure agreement, an airtight NDA you sign covering everything from the instant you met Catherine to what happened today and everything in between. Answer fast. I need to get back to my family."

"Sure," Alex sneered.

"I'm serious. Once this deal is done, no contact. And no more interviews." Edward's glare was dangerous.

"Hmm, big brother to the rescue? Yeah, I get it." Alex's mathematical wheels spun in his brain.

"Good. I'm sending the details of this agreement and a recording to my paralegal right now." Edward hit send, "Come to my office in the morning. Now get the hell out of here."

As Alex left, Edward went over to George. "Keep him out."

Cate stood in the doorway to Robbie's room, watching Scott thoughtfully console his distraught brother.

In her mind, she reflected on MeeMac's advice to survive the *raging storm* of life. Cate had no idea how to do any of it.

Chapter 26
A Ray of Hope

*I*t had been seven weeks since the shooting. To Cate's great relief, Kyle was steadily improving in health and responsiveness. Visiting him was an uplifting experience for everyone in the family.

Cate was reading, a small light shining on her book, the blinds obscuring the morning sun. The nurse entered and unceremoniously drew the blinds, flooding the room with bright sunlight. Kyle woke up with a start.

"What are you doing?" Cate protested.

"Dr. Trask needs to check Mr. Weston, and he has to be awake."

"You could do it less aggressively." Cate set down her book and stepped to Kyle's side. Kissing him, she asked, "Hi, honey, how are you feeling today?"

"Sleep deprivation should be considered a form of torture," he groaned.

The nurse left the room.

"Well, *Nurse Ratched* went to get the doctor."

Kyle glanced at the door. "Where's George?"

"I wasn't doing much today, so I gave him the day off."

"That's not the protocol, honey. I know you don't enjoy the invasion of privacy, but I want you and the kids safe."

"It's over. She's gone. Do I even need security anymore?"

"Until I'm with you, yes!" He saw how thin she was getting. "How are you?"

"I'm fine. We all are. Ed's taking care of everything. He won't let me do anything, which is unnerving. I hate not being in charge of my own life." She sat on the edge of the bed.

"He's doing what I asked him to do. Are you eating?"

"Strange question." She adjusted his pillow.

"You're really thin, honey. Please, don't make me worry."

"I don't have much of an appetite," she shrugged.

Kyle touched her cheek, looking earnestly at her. "Sweetheart, I don't want anything to happen to you."

"I miss you so much." Cate laid down on the bed beside him. "I can't sleep without you." He swept her hair from her eyes as she continued. "The other morning, Mia crawled in the bed with me to watch Saturday morning cartoons like we used to do together. She complained the bed was too big because Daddy wasn't there. Everybody misses you."

"Well, here's some good news." He pulled himself up with the bars over his bed. "I have feeling again in my lower back, they have me wiggling my toes, and I'm getting a fair amount of mobility in my legs. I think the doctor plans to transfer me to a physical rehabilitation facility."

"Good news? Kyle, that's fantastic!" Cate sat up, thrilled.

"As a matter of fact, ouch … sweetheart, you're on my leg." Kyle flinched from the pain.

Cate's leg was slightly lying across one of Kyle's. "Oh, my. Sorry, honey. Let me get off the bed."

As Cate made her way to the chair, Dr. Trask entered.

"Hello, Mr. and Mrs. Weston. How are you this morning, Kyle?"

"Stronger, doctor." Kyle pulled himself up a bit straighter.

"Good. Well, let's see how we're doing, shall we?"

Cate picked up her bag and book and started to leave. "I'm running some errands. Kyle, do you need anything? Anything I can bring you?"

"Yes, would you please run by the production office? Ruth has some material for me to review. She's been asking to come by. I'd rather you bring it to me."

"Of course, no problem. I love you, honey." Cate rested her hand on the door handle.

"Love you too."

"Take care of my husband, doctor," she cautioned with a grin.

"Catherine, I promise," Dr. Trask smiled.

A wave of contentment came over Cate. Although she tried not to read too much into what Kyle had told her, how could she not rejoice? This was what she had been praying for since the first night. There was much more work, of course. Still, she could finally breathe easier.

Chapter 27
Suspension of Disbelief

*C*ate strolled from the Westlight Production offices with the information Kyle requested. She grasped why Kyle didn't want Ruth to bring them. Kyle was private regarding the extent of his condition. While he felt a need to be productive, he limited visitors to the family.

As Cate opened her car, a shadow passed her eyes.

"Catherine Leigh."

Cate turned to see Everett Franklin, one of the executives of the studios.

"Mr. Franklin, you startled me," said Cate, holding her hand over her heart.

"How are you, my dear?" Franklin touched her in a most unwanted manner, slyly running his hand up and down her upper arm.

"I'm doing well, thank you." Cate subtly pulled away from him, finding her phone and briefly thinking how stupid she had been not to have security.

"And how's Kyle?"

"He's doing much better. Thank you for your concern." She clutched the car door handle, devising how she could best make a getaway.

"Come up to my office," Franklin coerced, his distinctively creepy vibe on overload. "We need to finally have our meeting concerning your future here at the studio."

"Mr. Franklin, I'd like to, but I'm running late to pick up my daughter." An absolute lie Cate was compelled to tell. Lynn always brought Mia home from school. "Perhaps another time." Cate stepped back against her car.

"I'm sure you have a few minutes you can spare. This meeting's been put on hold long enough. It's important. This is not a request." He started to his office and detected a stall. He moved to her once again. "Now, Catherine." He extended his arm around her back, firmly pushing her toward his office door. Cate's heart pounded, and her palms began to sweat.

The reception area was empty. Franklin's assistant had left for the day, and they were alone in the dimly lit office. Cate held her phone, her mind cluttered.

"I heard you turned down an excellent role due to the incident. Appallingly fatal to a career," Franklin admonished.

"Kyle had been shot and was fighting for his life," Cate snapped, aghast at his comment. "I wasn't leaving my husband." Cate took a seat far away from him on the other side of his massive desk.

"Such a burden." He walked around his desk to sit on the corner, hanging over the chair where she sat.

"My husband's not a burden. He's a blessing." Her voice was firm, not betraying the fear rising in her. Cate held her phone slightly forward, her hands in her lap, discreetly toying with it.

"Admirable." Franklin approached her. "Maybe we can reward such loyalty." Cate jostled her chair further away. "Although, misplaced loyalty, don't you think?" He eyed her provocatively. "After all, he's not much of a husband anymore, is he?"

"I beg your pardon?" She stared at him, her past overpowering her rational mind. Then, forcibly regaining her bearings, she struggled to remain present.

"From what I hear, things aren't working. Must get lonely." His look burrowed through her.

"What's your point?" Cate shoved her chair away from him.

"We could work well together. There's a lot we could do to help each other." He advanced, grasping her armrests with both his hands, hemming her in.

"Mr. Franklin, this has been eye-opening. I need to pick up my child. The child I had with my husband. Excuse me." She wrestled to get by his arms, but he wouldn't release his hold.

"Certainly, someone else can pick up the kid. Don't you have a nanny who can help? Call. I insist. You haven't heard my well-endowed offer." He thrust his face within inches of hers.

"Oh, hell," she glared at him in revolting disbelief. "I'm listening." Cate adjusted her cell phone and faked texting a message.

"I see you having an active future, Catherine. I can open big doors for you. I could help. You're a skillful actress ... sexy ... with hidden talents. I need your best performances for me." Franklin heaved her out of the chair and held her chin. She froze, overpowered by memories flooding her mind of a distant time when she was young. Gradually, her mood changed, her mind rebelling. I survived a loaded gun pressing against my heart, she realized. After months of trauma, I'm steeled against adversity. I'm no longer a frightened schoolgirl.

Cate pulled her chin from Franklin's grip, angrily staring at him. "Are you going to chase me around the desk now?"

"Do you realize who you're speaking to?" Franklin roughly grabbed her chin again.

"Don't bully, don't touch me," she threatened, putting her hand on his face and pushing hard.

"This can end your career," growled Franklin, the common threat echoing from the rafters.

"I don't think so, Mr. Franklin. It'll end yours."

Franklin clenched her arms to pull her to him. Cate parried his grasp and shoved him back into the chair, confidently striding from the office, never giving him a second look.

At her car, Cate turned over the phone in her hand and sneered at the screen, which showed it had recorded the entire conversation. She clicked it off and yelled toward Everett Franklin's office window. "Take that, you son of a bitch."

Edward came out from behind his desk and sat next to Cate on his couch, holding her hand. She was exhausted.

"Geez, this recording's disgusting," he said. "What a scumbag. You okay, Sis?"

"Yeah, at first I was intimidated, and then I was mad." She rubbed her forehead. "What he said about Kyle ... ooh, I could have wrung his neck! What a bastard! What's our next move?"

"I'll file a complaint tomorrow. You want me to inform the unions, the studio?" He returned the phone to her.

"You can inform the entire world if you want. Just don't hurt my career, please. Franklin's career, I don't care. He deserves it."

"I've heard rumors for years about Franklin and his alleged harassments," said Edward. "I think there's at least one, maybe two instances that have already been reported. I should've warned you, Sis. I'm sorry."

"How were you supposed to know he'd be going after his number one box-office star's wife? Jerk. I want to make sure he regrets it."

"You're damn formidable, Sis." Edward smiled.

"Formidable? Yeah ... well, now anyway," Cate said, lowering her head.

"I'm proud of you." Edward gently squeezed her arm.

"Why? Impressed I didn't high-tail and run this time?" She lifted her head.

"Catherine, this is completely different." He rested his hand on her shoulder.

"You don't have to tell me. I know. I was young, naïve. I was ..." Cate placed her hands over her face. "I can't even ..."

Edward waffled, "Have ... have you told Kyle about it?"

"No, why would I?" She ran her hand through her hair, tugging on it in aggravation.

"Because he's your husband."

"Good reason not to." Cate glared up swiftly. "I told Alex and look what happened."

"Alex is an asshole. Kyle's not Alex."

"I've told two people in my life," Cate muttered. "You're the only one who cared."

"Because I love you, Sis." Edward positioned himself to make eye contact. "And you ought to tell Kyle."

"Why?"

"He's your husband … and best friend." Edward patted her hand.

"Maybe he shouldn't know."

"It would give Kyle the real reason why you left Hollywood and ran away to Alabama. And how courageous of you to come back to face it again and not let it drive you away."

"Ed, please," she whined, rubbing her forehead as if to erase the plague from her mind.

"Also, consider that you'd be sharing this part of yourself with the one person you truly trust … Kyle."

Somberly, Cate dropped down to the couch.

"Catherine, you're a grown woman," he continued, "and it's haunted you for years." Edward retook her hand. "Did you ever get help?"

"No, I kept hearing what Mom always preached … you got yourself into the mess; you get yourself out of it."

"That's such bullshit! I'm sorry you accepted it."

"Accepted it? I lived it." Cate stood and began to pace.

"It's time to let it go, Catherine. Tell Kyle."

"He'll see me differently."

"No, he won't. It's Kyle. He'll simply see your strength."

"How can you be sure?" Her eyes glazed over with a timid cast.

"I know who you are, my sweet sister. You did nothing wrong. It wasn't your fault. You were innocent. Still are. Please believe me."

Cate sat in deep contemplation. Finally, she looked up at Edward with a single laugh.

"Shit, big brother, I hate it when you're right."

Chapter 28
Hurdles and Locked Doors

K yle rested on a big, cushioned chair beside the picture window, reading a book. His room at the rehabilitation center was a nicely situated suite, looking out on a placid landscape featuring a fountain in the center of a small lake. Cate tapped on the door and entered.

"Hi," she smiled.

"Hi," he answered, hardly glimpsing from the book.

"I heard you had your first session today," she said with empathy and love. "It was tough, huh?"

He glanced away, holding back his words.

"I'm sorry, honey. I know it won't be easy, especially at first. If you need anything, I'm here."

He returned to his book.

Cate paused. His demeanor seemed crushingly forlorn. What could she do? Compassion poured from her mind, aching to somehow make things better for him. Cate knelt, hoping to influence him to see her.

"The room's cozy. Anything from home I can bring?"

"No, thank you," he mumbled.

"Well, I'll bring the children by tomorrow after school. They miss you so much."

"No, Cate." Kyle looked up, fearful. "I don't want anyone to come here. Just you, okay?"

"You don't want to see your children?" Confusion shaded her face.

"Please. No, not like this," Kyle said, indicating the wheelchair and various medical equipment. "No one, please. I'll be home soon enough."

There was a long silence between them. Cate swallowed hard, fighting the despair.

"All right, I'll see you in the morning. Get some rest." She took his hand and kissed him on the cheek. "I love you, Kyle."

He tightened his grip on her hand and wouldn't release it. She felt an expectancy that perhaps he wanted to ask something … for her to stay so he could bare his soul. Their vision met.

Her instincts were correct. Kyle did long to open his heart to her, but his intentions were scattered, unforgiving hurdles muting his words.

"I love you, Catie," he eventually said.

Holding his face in her hands, she kissed him.

"I love you," he repeated.

"I do too," she said softly. "See you tomorrow, love."

After she left, Kyle gaped vacantly, his mind drifting to what once was … to hold his wife, to make love to her. It felt like a distant dream.

Chapter 29
Confessional

*T*wo months after entering the rehab facility, Kyle was cleared by his doctors to continue physical therapy from home. Although he was getting stronger, he was hesitant, insisting he stay at the facility. Cate didn't understand why, and Kyle was stalwart not to explain.

Although he cherished his time with Cate, he still refused to see anyone else. The children were dismayed and hurt. How she wished to rationalize his decision, especially to Scott, who had taken on the mantle of being the man of the house.

Cate was about to enter Westlight Productions, her weekly trip to retrieve material for Kyle to keep his mind busy.

"Cate," a voice called out.

She turned to see an old friend walking toward her.

"Joseph!" She ran over and threw her arms around him, unable to hide her sadness.

"Everything all right?" He held her a tad away from him to meet her glance.

"I don't know," she answered glumly.

"Come with me. Let's get some lunch."

They sat at a corner table in the near-empty commissary, the lunch crowd gone. Cate sat wordlessly, picking at her uneaten sandwich.

"Cate, what's going on? I can't help unless you tell me."

Cate tentatively pushed her plate away. "Physical therapy's progressing, but he doesn't want anyone else to visit. Phoning is fine. He'll only see me. Kyle says he needs to work on his healing alone, and frankly, it's rocking us to the core."

"Even the kids?"

She nervously brushed the crumbs from the tablecloth. "Yes, it's tearing them up. They need him. They must believe he's there for them no matter what. And I know he is. The boys, especially, feel shut out. It's as if everything's falling apart." She took a long, sad breath. "He doesn't want them to see him struggling. Like he's supposed to be superhuman, and if they saw, they'd know he's just a man. He underestimates them, Joseph."

She placed her hands under her knees and hung her head down, an old habit of uneasiness.

"He underestimates you too." Joseph sipped his water.

Cate's eyes cut upward. "What do you mean?"

Joseph gave an uncomfortable smile, repressing his words.

"From the beginning," she continued, "I strived to make the family a strong, caring unit. Over the last few years, Kyle was taking more time for everyone. The kids loved the attention. Now, I'm afraid we'll never be the same again."

"Cate, nothing will ever be the same," Joseph said sympathetically.

Cate stared at Joseph with horror, a cold chill ramping across her being as she briefly relived the attack.

"This *is* a life-changing event," he clarified. "It doesn't mean it'll be worse. It can be better, even happier. Value your time together more."

Joseph sat back and added casually, "I've seen him."

"What? How?"

"Since when have rules ever stopped me," he smiled. "I went and sat with him for a while. He didn't do a lot of talking. I understood, even empathized."

"What did he say?"

Joseph paused, realizing he was in a tough spot. He couldn't share the secrets of one friend with another, even if revealing them would comfort her.

"Cate, I've never known two people love each other more. It's inspiring to the rest of us jokers searching for meaning in a one-night stand. And the kids, Kyle cherishes them. The love he has for all of you doesn't simply vanish. He'll come around. Trust it."

Joseph took a big bite out of his sandwich, and mumbled with a full mouth, "Now eat something, will you, before you blow away, skinny girl."

Chapter 30
The Star and the Actress

T om handed Cate a cup of tea and a script.
"Read it. You need to work again. It'll keep your mind busy."

"I can't leave him now."

"It shoots here in town. No locations. It's a good part. A comedy. You could use some levity in your life." Tom tapped his pencil on his desk while he spoke.

"I'm not feeling funny lately."

"You're an actor. Act funny." Tom shuffled a stack of scripts on his desk. "How's he doing? How's physical therapy?"

"Okay, I guess. I wish Kyle would come home. The medical staff says he can have a PTA come to the house. But he thinks he'll improve faster if he stays there."

"So, give him space, Cate, and work. It'll help everybody."

Tom peeked at her, brimming with anticipation. "I have other news. There's talk about giving you a star on the Walk of Fame."

"No." Cate set down the script.

"What, do you mean no?" Tom asked, confused.

"No, not before Kyle," she stuttered.

"Cate, Kyle's getting his dedication. They're simply waiting until he's up and around and can come to the ceremony. In the meantime, they want to present you with yours right away. I think the incident at the museum has made you both national icons."

"No. His first. I'll wait. Kyle won an Oscar. He's the star in our family … he's the true celebrity." Cate counted off all her husband's accomplishments. "Tom, Kyle's not just an icon. He's a hero! I'm only an actress." Cate silently shook her head.

"You've won an Oscar, too, Cate. It's time you accept who you are. An extraordinary talent, a name."

"No star on the Walk of Fame until Kyle has his and, ideally, a long time after," she ordered, abruptly standing, and beginning to pace. "Please don't even mention this to him, Tom."

"I won't if you promise you'll consider the script."

"When does this shoot?"

"In two weeks."

"Let me sleep on it. I'll let you know in the morning." She opened the door and said with a twinkle, "I'll probably do it."

"You *are* a star." Tom smiled.

Cate stretched out on the sofa, watching a DVD, Oakley snuggling beside her. It was the kiss scene that Sy Barnes had sneakily filmed seven years ago when they shot *Sunset Rise*. She closely studied her reaction to Kyle's passionate kiss, her mind on overdrive. Goodness, she contemplated; why didn't I say how I felt right then? I was a fool not to admit I loved him so much … my heart and soul were his.

"Mom, hey, I've got some news," Scott yelled as he opened the front door to the beach house. Oakley leaped from the sofa, practically knocking Scott down with his greeting.

Cate paused the player.

"Hi, sweetie," Cate responded, hastily sitting up and wiping tear-stained cheeks with her sleeve. "What is it?"

Petting Oakley, Scott tapped into the solemn tempo in the house. "Where's everybody?"

"Robbie's out with his friends, and Lynn took Mia to a birthday party."

"So, what's on TV?" He inclined over the sofa beside her.

"It's an outtake from *Sunset Rise*," she replied casually.

"I don't remember that scene."

"No, it was never used." Cate quickly changed the subject. "So, tell me, what is it?"

Scott held out a letter, his face glowing. "I've been accepted to Notre Dame."

"Oh, how marvelous, sweetheart. I'm so proud of you." Cate jumped from the sofa and hugged him.

"I'm doing the accelerated program. Class of 2019. And then I'm hoping to go to law school."

"So, Uncle Ed hasn't scared you away?" Cate smiled.

"You know how much I love my internship at the firm," Scott laughed. "Uncle Ed assured me I can do it again next summer. I think the law's fascinating."

"That's great, honey. What did your mom say when you told her?"

"I haven't told my mom." Scott took an exerted breath and plopped down beside her; his delight dampened. "She won't be happy that I'm halfway across the country."

"Honey, I'll miss the heck out of you. You're my rock. And I know Robbie and Mia will be lost without you. But this is something you must do for yourself. Every child has to grow up and venture away from home. It's part of life. Julia loves you, and she'll be lonely without you, but I have a hunch she'll understand. Go. Discover your dreams, have adventures, live life." She lightly tickled him. "Safely, please."

"I knew you'd be happy for me, Mom."

"Julia will be happy for you, too. I guarantee it."

"What about Dad?"

"Of course he'll be pleased," she grinned. "Oh, Scott, a lawyer ... so exciting!"

Scott took a relaxing breath, studying his stepmom. "Can I say something, Mom?"

"Sure, sweetheart." She probed with a chuckle, "Should I be worried?"

"Never," Scott smiled. "I think you already know this, but in my opinion, you were the missing piece in the family. You made my dad a better man, a better father."

Deeply touched, for a moment Cate was unable to speak.

"Honey, you're such an extraordinary young man," she finally responded, unable to fight back the tears. "So wise and sensitive and kind ... such a generous spirit." Cate silently was reminded Scott's best qualities were gleaned from Kyle.

Starting to feel a bit misty himself, Scott needed to redirect the conversation. "So, how's Dad?"

"Getting better. They're working him hard in physical therapy."

"Mom, I need to visit him. Talking on the phone is stupid."

With no words to comfort him, she forced a poignant expression, her hand cupping his face. "He'll come home soon."

Turning away, Scott glanced at the frozen figures on the TV screen. "Mom, I haven't seen *Sunset Rise* in a while. Why don't we watch it? I'll make some popcorn."

She kissed him on the cheek and said with a laugh, "I'd like some butter on mine, please." Scott's eyes shone with contentment. Cate was one of his favorite people.

Chapter 31
The Measure of a Man

*E*ven a basic workout felt strenuous, but Kyle regularly ramped up his sessions, including weights to increase muscle mass. He was exhausted, battling to push his legs forward for the day's last set on the leg press.

Scott stood near the doorway out of sight, pained to see his father fight his own body.

"Well done, Kyle," rallied Luke, the physical therapist. "It's enough for today. You worked hard. I know you'd rather not but please take your pain medicine tonight. It'll help you to get some rest."

Kyle had graduated from the walker to two canes. Luke guided him toward the hallway back to his room. Scott stepped out of sight and into the darkness of the corner so his father wouldn't see him when he walked by.

When they arrived at Kyle's room, Luke said goodbye for the day. Kyle strived to open the door, and Scott came around the corner.

"Let me help you, Dad." Scott took Kyle's arm.

"Scott?" Kyle was surprised, allowing Scott to help him transfer to a big chair in front of the picture window, viewing the fountain in the lake.

"Hey, Dad. You're looking good." Scott inspected the room. "I need to talk to you, Dad. Face to face."

"Okay," Kyle answered timidly.

Scott wasn't delaying why he came. "When are you coming home?"

"I don't know." Kyle stared out the window, his mind torn by an emotional war ... the overpowering urge to embrace his son; the hardhearted distress to push him away.

"Dad, you have to come home. It's not about missing you, which we do. It's because it's time. Mom can't do this alone. And honestly, Rob and I are worried about Mom. She doesn't eat. She doesn't sleep. She hovers over us, especially Mia. Rob and Mia need you, Dad."

"And you, Scott?"

"First, I want to tell you I love you, Dad ... I do," Scott assertively answered. "But what I'm about to say will seem harsh. It's something I've needed to say to you since I was little."

Kyle watched Scott intently.

"It struck me talking to Mom the other day at the beach house. Since I was little, I was fully aware your career and, frankly, the women you were with meant so much more than I did. It hurt, and I was angry for years. I was glad I lived with my mom and not you. Because I felt I wasn't important to you. I can't tell you how sad it is for a little boy to think his father doesn't care unless it's convenient, in between movies and girlfriends."

Scott took a deep breath to hold back his emotions. "One of the best days of my life was when you met Cate. You changed because of her. Cate made you a good father by her being a great mother. Cate was more special to me than you were during those early days. I knew *she* loved me. She became my parent. The one I was missing." Scott paused. "Dad, she literally saved my life."

Glimpsing at his father's distraught expression, Scott knew he must moderate his honesty.

"Dad, I'm not saying this to hurt you. You're a wonderful father now. And I'm so relieved. Just know there's a huge gap in our family without you. Mom needs you, Dad. It's time to leave this place."

Kyle's eyes were glassy, holding back his regret.

Scott touched his dad's arm, "Be our father again. Come home, Dad." Scott hugged his father.

"I'm so sorry, Scott," Kyle said softly, his voice nearly cracking. "I've always loved you."

"I know, Dad."

Entering from the garage, Cate abruptly stopped. The kitchen looked like a tornado had hit—dirty pots and pans overflowing from the sink, chopped vegetables strewn across the center island, the refrigerator door wide open.

"Mommy," Mia shouted, "Robbie's cooking chicken fajitas."

"Great timing," said the chef. "Dinner's almost ready."

"Wow, this is a pleasant surprise," said Cate, searching for a spot to set her purse. "Such a treat. Looks like you made everything from scratch."

"I did, even the salsa. And I made enough for Uncle Ed. He's on his way."

"So nice of you." Cate sat on the island bar stool and kicked off her shoes. "Where's Scott tonight?"

"He's at his …" Robbie glanced at Mia. "He's at Aunt Julia's house."

"Scott's always with Aunt Julia," Mia pouted while rummaging through the refrigerator to find a drink.

"Yeah, Mia. Strange, isn't it?" Robbie teased. "You explain, Mom."

"Nothing to explain, Robert." Cate glared at her fourteen-year-old son. "Mia, Scott loves Aunt Julia, and when your dad gets home, we'll explain it to you."

"I love Aunt Julia, but I like being with you, Mommy." The doorbell broke Mia's thoughts. "I'll get it," she screamed, racing Oakley to the door.

Edward walked into the kitchen and stepped close to Cate.

"We need to talk, alone." He gestured toward Mia and Robbie, his stare signaling they shouldn't be a party to the conversation. Cate turned pale.

"Sorry, Sis." Edward quelled her fears, "Kyle's fine."

Cate took a breath. "Oh, Ed, don't scare me. Let's go out onto the deck."

The night sky was starless against the full moon shimmering on the ocean waves. It was a still night with a cooling breeze.

"What is it?"

"I had a call from Joseph Beason today." Edward led her to the far corner of the deck, away from the doors. "Kyle's ready to come home except …" Edward sat on the railing.

"Except what?" Cate moved over to him.

"He's concerned about how permanent the paralysis is."

Cate was baffled. "What does he mean? They have him up and walking. I think he's moving around pretty well."

Edward grappled to secure the right words. "I think he's not regained all functionalities."

Cate gaped at him, bewildered.

"Catherine, please get what I'm saying. It's awkward for me to counsel my sister on her sex life."

"Oh, my," Cate said, shocked. "Ed, it doesn't matter. Kyle and I are so much more than that."

"It matters to him. Which means it has to matter to you. Hey, it's the male psyche. The medical prognosis has been good. Know it's probably emotional, not physical. The doctors convinced him he needs to come home and deal with it."

"Thank you." She meekly smiled.

"Talking about your sex life is not something I ever want to do again," he bristled. "At least it wasn't as bad as watching *Piercing Heat* … your transformation into such a free-spirited woman."

"Stop it, Ed," she laughed. "It was a tough role for me on many levels." They opened the doors to enter the living room. The table was set and ready for dinner.

"I know, Sis," he said, gazing at her sincerely. "It astonished me you were able to handle it."

"What can Mom handle, Uncle Ed?" Robbie asked, overhearing the end of their conversation.

"We were discussing your mom's Oscar award-winning performance and how I saw my kid sister in a whole new light," Edward winced.

"You know the love scene, Uncle Ed? They used a body double. Dad told Scott and me." Robbie jumped up and rushed to the kitchen. "Oops, forgot the tortillas."

Edward put his elbows on the table, and his hands folded in front of him, confidentially, with a big brother *I'm-gonna-tell-Mom* glare. "Sister, so a body double, huh?"

"Brother, it's what my husband told his sons." Cate narrowed her eyes at him.

"Fascinating. Hated that picture in my head," he smirked.

"I hate it in anyone's head."

Chapter 32
Catch Me When I Fall

fter nearly five months, Kyle was home. The physical therapist had requested Cate to not be *too* helpful. Kyle had to be self-reliant, accomplishing everyday tasks unaided.

"I need a chair," Kyle advised, cautiously reaching the sofa, canes guiding his effort. "This looks cozy, but what if I can't get out of it?"

"That's why we have Scott and Robbie," she said glibly, fighting the urge to support him.

"If I get stuck, maybe Ed will bring them home," Kyle chuckled.

"They'll be here in the morning," said Cate, closely watching his every movement. "I figured the kids spending the night at Ed's would allow you to acclimate to the house before their exuberance, particularly Mia, overtook you. And, mostly, I thought it would be nice for us to be alone."

She moved to him and rubbed his arm as he gingerly transferred his weight and lowered himself into a chair.

"This is difficult, Cate."

"What? Being home?"

"All of it. Being here, being this way." He glanced down at his body.

"It'll take time, sweetheart, but we have all the time in the world. You're doing so well, and we're together now." She bent forward to kiss him gently. She ran her fingers through his hair and gazed lovingly at him, kissing him again. Her embrace became more earnest and desirous.

"It's been so long," Kyle whispered, drawing her closer to him, passion engulfing them. After a few minutes, Kyle pushed away, holding Cate's arm to get her to look at him.

"I'm not sure I can do this," he said nervously.

Cate sat on the edge of her chair and held both of his hands. "It's okay. We'll take it slow."

He looked down at the floor.

"I'm so happy to be with my best friend," she shined, giving him a light kiss.

Kyle did not move, his mind frightened and confused. Could he make love … ever again? Of course, he could. But what if he couldn't?

Sensing the depth of his worry, Cate noticed a movie flyer on the end table.

"We need to go to the movies," she said, her voice almost too perky. "There are some really good new releases I'd like to see. And I'm craving theater popcorn and cuddling in the balcony with you."

He studied her kindhearted efforts, reliving the old days when they were united by the truest of friendships. He touched her cheek with the back of his hand, adoringly taking in her beauty.

"Cate, can we please go to bed? I need to hold you."

"Yes, please." She stood, handing him the two canes. "Ready?"

Together, they carefully walked to the bedroom.

The bed was restful again. It had been months since Cate could fall asleep. They both slept soundly in each other's arms all night. The dawn broke, and Cate lazily awoke to absorb the scene. Cate was happy. She had Kyle. There was work ahead, yet together they could do the impossible.

It felt serene, his body against hers, bound and warm. Cate watched him sleep.

She sat up in bed and giggled to herself.

"Kyle, you still asleep?" She said quietly.

"I was," he grumbled, trying to cling to his state of unconsciousness.

"What are you dreaming?" She spoke tenderly.

"About us. My New Orleans' dream and the white cotton dress you wore. Hmm …"

"Good dream, huh?"

"Yeah, the best." He had an exaggerated grin on his face.

"I noticed," Cate said offhandedly.

"Yeah? What do you mean?" He strained against the morning light to see her.

With a puckish glint in her eyes, Cate cleared her throat and pointed down toward his groin, where the covers were poking up.

Kyle pushed himself up. "Well, damn."

"You can say that again. Now, are your worries eliminated about things not working?"

Kyle rolled to his side and pulled Cate to him. "Maybe I should've come home sooner?"

"Uh-huh." She nuzzled closer. "You need to tell me about that dream."

"Why don't I show you?" He kissed her passionately.

The loud bang of the front door slamming caused them to break off their clinch.

"Mom, Dad, we're home," Robbie yelled from the kitchen.

"Daddy," Mia hollered.

Cate and Kyle gazed at each other longingly, and Kyle said, "To be ..."

"Continued," Cate finished and rolled out of bed to her husband's sincere disappointment.

"It's probably prudent we're waiting," said Cate, putting on her robe. "I'll make some breakfast." She added with a laugh, "Would you like me to turn on a cold shower for you?"

Chapter 33
Glow of Dawn

The shattering boom of thunder and a blinding streak of lightning startled Cate as she hastened to empty the refrigerator contents into the three large coolers full of ice. Power was out across much of the Los Angeles area. Edward had taken refuge at his sister's since he was hopelessly unprepared for an outage and knew Cate possessed the magic to whip up something delicious out of whatever may be in the refrigerator. Everyone was endeavoring to entertain Mia, who was beyond fidgety since she couldn't watch her favorite movie, *Beauty and the Beast*.

The front door swung open, and Scott entered from the torrential storm.

"Sweetie," Cate greeted Scott, "what a pleasant surprise. I didn't think we'd see you until next week."

"I was caught in this mess, and it was easier to get here than to Mom's."

Mia pranced up to Scott to correct him. "This is Mom's."

"Excuse me, Mia. I meant Aunt Julia's."

"One day, we have to explain it to her. She's five," Robbie volunteered. "I'd be happy to tell her."

"Not today, Robert," Cate chastised. "Scott, you did call Julia to let her know you're safe, didn't you?"

"Yes, Mom, I did," Scott assured, taking a small device from his coat pocket. "Hey, Mia, look what I have. My portable Blu-ray player, all charged up."

"Yay!" Mia grabbed it from Scott and, together with Oakley, ran to her bedroom, slamming the door.

"Well, we won't see her the rest of the night," Kyle laughed.

"Join us, Scott." Cate walked back into the living room.

Scott moved over to where Robbie stood off to the side.

"What's all the bull? You were already at your mom's." Robbie mumbled to Scott.

"I wanted to be here for moral support, and I knew we had to keep Mia busy," Scott said in a low voice. "Dude, don't look so worried."

"Dad. Mom, Uncle Ed," Scott called. "Rob has something he wants to talk to us about."

"Go on." Scott nudged Robbie and Edward grinned shrewdly, placing a manila envelope on the coffee table.

"Okay," Robbie began with a nervous smile. "Well, we're the Weston family. Except I'm not. I'm a Miller. And I don't feel connected to that name." Robbie took a bold breath, looking to Kyle. "Dad, I want to be a Weston, if it's all right? Officially."

Kyle was stunned.

"Dad, I think it's great." Scott confirmed, "Rob's always been my brother."

Kyle was overcome with pride. "Rob, I'd be honored if you shared my name."

Cate gazed between them with joy bubbling inside her.

"Good," said Edward. "I assume it was an astute decision on Rob's part to retain counsel to prepare these legal documents for the name change." Edward opened the envelope and passed the papers to Kyle and Cate for their review and signatures.

"Everything's ready to file in court except the exact way you'd prefer your name," Edward announced. "Robert Weston. Any middle name?"

"You don't already have a middle name?" Scott posed, shocked.

"No, sweetie. Robbie's dad and I could never agree on one," Cate budged uneasily.

As Robbie examined the room full of anticipating faces, he paused on his uncle's.

"Edward," Robbie spoke with conviction. "Robert Edward Weston."

Edward glanced from the family to his nephew. Misty-eyed as he wrote the name, he was too choked up to speak.

Chapter 34
A Stroke of Genius

R elaxing on the deck, Cate felt the sun's heat on her body, her thoughts drifting back seven years to their honeymoon in Tahiti. She could recreate every second …

She and Kyle had been sunning on the private deck of their yacht. Cate wore a new bikini, a surprise gift from Kyle.

"I like how sexy you are in that swimsuit," Kyle had flirted.

"Do you now?" She giggled.

"It fits you extremely well." He ran his fingers up and down her back. "And you won't have many tan lines."

"I never have *any* tan lines." She rubbed sunscreen on her arms.

"Huh? What do you mean?"

"My secret's simple. I go to the health club and stand in the tanning booth naked to even out my tan. Voilà, no tan lines."

"Catherine Weston." He pushed his hat up and gawked at her.

"What? I've done it for years."

"There's a picture you should never have put in my mind." He leaned over and kissed her fervently.

Cate opened her eyes. The memory was so tangible she could almost feel the kiss even now.

Kyle, using both canes, carefully meandered from the main living area to the deck.

"Hello, my love." He sat next to her, holding her hand to kiss it.

"You're looking better," she uttered.

"It's getting easier." He sighed, and she tightened her grip, leaning over to kiss him on the cheek.

"So, darling," she said, "are you feeling up to taking on a project?"

"Work?"

"It might be good for you."

"In front of the camera?"

"I wasn't suggesting in front of the camera."

"I hate office work," he scowled. "Sitting at the production company would drive me crazy."

"I wasn't proposing that either. What about directing?" Cate sat up and hung her legs over the side.

"Directing?"

"You've been intimately involved with nearly every aspect of production since you began Westlight. You'd be great."

"I don't know, Catie." He narrowed his eyes, searching her expression. "Honestly?"

"Yes, you're a born director, Kyle. You've always given me insightful directions on set. I could never have done *Elk Crossing* or *Sunset Rise* without your guidance. *Piercing Heat* ... no way I would've won an Oscar without you motivating me."

"Is that a nice way of saying I was pushing you?" He grinned.

"Not pushing," Cate laughed. "Strong directing."

"Where do I even start?" He yanked his hat lower, his face nearly covered.

Cate lifted a script from the small outdoor table and plopped it on his lap.

"Wait," he said. "Isn't this the project Tom sent to you?" He pushed up his cap and sat straight.

"No, it's your favorite TV show, *Concrete Calvary*, and they've requested you direct an episode this season. Tom picked this one. There are others to choose from, though."

"Television?" Turning the script over and over, he was immersed in ideas.

"It's a place to get your feet wet and find out if you enjoy directing."

Kyle looked over the pages, the corners of his mouth brightening into a smile.

"Well, I persuaded you to do the movie where you won an Oscar," he said. "I guess it's fair play."

"So, I've talked you into it?"

"I'm intrigued," he nodded. "You're smooth."

Without hesitation, Cate found her phone and hit a button.

"Hey, Tom, it's Cate. He'll do it … I'm glad too … Thanks." She dramatically clicked off the phone and set it down.

"You planned this?"

"Of course." She gave him an ardent kiss. "I love you."

Chapter 35
Westlight

Feeling like a stranger, Kyle opened the door to the Westlight offices. Ruth was in a conversation with the receptionist. They both turned and let out screams of elation. The rest of the office staff stuck their heads out to see the disruption, and everyone ran toward him. Ruth was the fastest, throwing her arms around Kyle, pushing everyone else away.

"Don't crowd him," she ordered, the group swarming to share their welcomed hellos. "Kyle, this is so exciting. We've missed you."

"Thanks, Ruth. And thanks, everyone. Believe me, I'm so happy to be back."

As the noise level heightened, Kyle lifted his cane. "Okay, gang, I'm humbled by this terrific reception, but I have about seven months of work to catch up on and hopefully enough energy to make it safely to my desk."

Kyle methodically followed Ruth to his office, and the staff enthusiastically returned to their stations.

"So, bring me up to speed," he said, stopping to laugh as she opened the door for him. "I see the work on my desk didn't disappear."

"Well, a lot of it did," she grinned. "You've been getting the material and scripts I sent over?"

"Yeah, good stuff. The only thing I didn't read was the tabloids and trades. It was a nice vacation from the garbage."

"You do know about Everett Franklin?"

"No, is he okay?"

"Probably not. Several actresses have accused him of everything from sexual harassment to rape. The word is he'll be fired if he doesn't resign first, and then who knows? Apparently, the DA's building a strong case."

"Wow, I *have* been out of the loop. This happened while I was in the hospital?" Kyle adjusted his posture to relax in his chair and set his cane to the side.

"Well, it's been occurring for more than a decade. It came to the surface when … didn't Cate tell you anything about this?" Ruth glared questioningly.

"No, why?"

"Well, I would've imagined … maybe you should ask Cate."

"Ruth, what's going on?" Kyle moved forward, furrowing his brow.

Ruth opened the door wider and started to step out. "You know, I really need to get back to work. Can I get you anything?"

"Ruth, stop, please."

Ruth froze and tentatively turned back.

"What do you know?" Kyle asked sternly.

Taking a deep breath to overcome her slip, Ruth revealed, "It was Cate. Franklin called her to his office and made vile suggestions from what I heard. She recorded it all. Her brother took it up the chain, and the authorities became involved. Once the word was out, several other actresses came forward with their stories. Some heartbreaking ones."

Kyle sat with his elbows on his desk, his hand covering his mouth.

"Cate's pretty special to all of us," Ruth stated. "What she did took a lot of courage."

Kyle let out a sigh and stared at Ruth. "It's the first I've heard of it."

"Kyle, with all you were going through, she probably didn't want to worry you."

"I'm not worried. I want to kill the bastard." Kyle exhaled to restrain his anger.

"Well, maybe that's the reaction she was trying to spare you," Ruth chuckled, opening the office door to leave. "Let me know if you need anything."

Kyle gazed out the window.

"Been away too long," he said to himself.

Chapter 36
There's No Place Like Home

The first chill of winter heightened Montana's splendor. The greens were muted by the cover of white fluffy snow falling ever so gently on the trees, rolling hills, and rooftops. The travelers—the Westons, Julia and John, Edward, and Emily—arrived full of energy and expectation. Oakley outraced them to the front door.

Having dramatically improved, Kyle now moved without a cane. Although he was still limited in some activities, such as horseback riding, the ranch had a curative, revitalizing effect on him. This was Kyle's paradise, designed and completed by Cate.

"Oh, it's nice to be home," Cate cooed, clutching Kyle's arm. Robbie and Scott led their cousin, Emily, to her guest room.

"Holy shit," Edward gawked at the grandeur before him. The welcoming foyer, the eighteen-foot ceilings with a massive fireplace and marble floors, the long hallways leading to the bedrooms.

"Ed!" Cate covered Mia's ears.

"Oh, sorry, Uncle Ed's a little overwhelmed. This is a lot to take in at first sight."

Kyle made his way into the living room. "Mia, come quick! Look."

A giant twelve-foot Christmas tree was in front of the grand picture window with an expansive view of the lake. The lights were strung, ornaments glistened, and a twinkly star graced the top.

Mia stood transfixed with a cherub look of glee, then dashed out of the room. "Robbie, Scottie, come see! Emi, come here!"

Cate murmured to Kyle with a wink, "Trust me. This will be the perfect Christmas."

Christmas night was magical, a blustery snow outside the windows, moonlight spilling through the clouds. Santa had been good to the eager kids, now in their rooms still sifting through their gifted haul. The adults relaxed near the roaring fire, wine in hand, with the only light coming from the twinkling tree and the fire's glow.

"Kyle, this is an incredible home." John snuggled with Julia on one sofa.

"It's Cate's design."

"Wait," said Edward. "You built this during *Elk Crossing*, way before you two were married."

"That's right. Construction took about ten months. It sat empty for a little while."

Scott came out of his room with Robbie, overhearing the discussion.

"Little while?" bellowed Scott. "We slept on mattresses on the floor for months. Cate picked out all the furniture and Dad had it waiting stuffed in the rec room and the gym for her to set it up when she and Rob came here."

Scott sat next to his mom.

Robbie sat on the arm of the other sofa near Cate. "Yeah, the movers loved how Mom kept changing her mind and making them carry the same furniture from one room to another," he shared.

Emily crept in and took a seat beside her father. Edward handed her his wine to sip. "Mia's finally asleep," Emily announced. "It took the second go-round of *Beauty and the Beast*."

Emily stretched her back. "What are you all talking about?"

"About how your Uncle Kyle can't design a home or pick out furniture," Edward goaded to a touch of jeers and laughter.

"Emily, I can do those things," Kyle amended. "I wanted your Aunt Catherine to realize her dream and know it was always here waiting for her."

"Scott told me the story," Emily smiled. "You built this for Aunt Catherine before you were together."

"Yes, and I didn't tell her until I almost lost her." Kyle kissed Cate's hand.

"You'd never lose me." Cate tilted her head, reassuring him.

"So, you told her about this place, and then you asked her to marry you?" John confirmed.

"I'd marry you if you built me a mansion." Edward scoffed, and everyone laughed.

Cate grinned, "I was stunned."

"Really, Mom? Even I figured it out, and I was what, seven?" Robbie asserted.

"Shh," Cate shushed Robbie. "What I was going to say is that it was a big surprise, but it wasn't the reason I said yes."

"What was it?" Kyle gazed at Cate, intrigued.

"I loved you," She vowed, sliding beneath his arm.

"Ugh, romance," Robbie fidgeted.

Kyle smiled, glancing at Julia, who was contently cuddling with John. They nodded back at him. Noticing the exchange, Cate knew it had been a wise decision to have the extended family together for the holidays.

All enjoyed the beauty and warmth of the Weston spread. The guests rode horses, and the kids built elaborate snowmen. Everyone took strolls around the lake or had fun at the outdoor fire pit. The week quickly went by.

Julia, John, Scott, Edward, and Emily would be leaving the following morning.

Packing his bag, Scott turned to Cate, who brought freshly washed clothes for his suitcase.

"Mom?" Scott took his stepmother's hand. "Thank you for inviting my mom and John here for Christmas. It was the best Christmas I think I've ever had."

Cate hugged Scott. "I'm glad we were together. It was my best Christmas too. I love you, sweetheart."

"I love you too, Mom."

It was quite late. Almost everyone had turned in when Cate entered the library, overhearing Kyle and Edward conversing in hushed tones. Straining to make out what was being discussed, she snuck in, hidden from view, until she heard Edward declare, "No, I did it for my sister and my nephew."

Not able to contain her curiosity, she called, "You did what for Robbie and me?"

Kyle buried his bearings on the drink in his hand, and Edward stuttered, "Ahh, what I always do. Watch out for you both."

Cate studied each of them.

"What's going on?" No one spoke. Cate sat down next to Edward on the loveseat, opposite Kyle.

"Kyle?"

Kyle took a sip from his glass.

"Ed?"

Silence.

"Someone say something," Cate charged, more than a little frustrated.

Kyle motioned to Edward.

Edward glared at Kyle. "It defeats the whole purpose of what I did."

"I think he already took care of that for you," Kyle pointed out.

"You both are driving me crazy. Please tell me." Cate was annoyed.

"Okay," said Kyle, "did you notice Robbie's trust account balance is whole again?"

"I did. I assumed you funded it once you were home from the hospital."

"No, I didn't know anything about it. Ed deposited eighty-thousand dollars of his own money."

Cate was overcome with affection, "Ed, honey, you didn't have to do that."

"I hated the idea of Robbie suffering for being a big-hearted kid. It's not Robbie's fault he has an asshole for a father."

"We'll pay you back," Cate confirmed.

"I already offered," said Kyle.

"No, he's my nephew. He's like my own son. It's my gift to him."

Cate smiled lovingly at her brother. "Ed, thank you."

"Oh, it gets better from there," Kyle interjected. "Tell her what else you did, Ed."

Edward groaned and set his drink down on the table. "I negotiated an agreement with an NDA to make sure Alex never bothers you or Robbie ever again."

Kyle quickly exclaimed, "For the mere price of two hundred and fifty thousand dollars of his money!"

"What the hell!" Cate gaped between the two of them, her mind bouncing from disbelief to confusion. "Why, when … when did all of this happen? Where was I?"

"It's when your ex-husband made his impromptu visit to the beach house," Edward explained. "After seeing how destroyed Robbie was, and you had to put up with Alex's bullshit, I had to do something. You were in no condition to handle one more crisis. He had to go. It was efficient. And I'm a good lawyer. It's an air-tight NDA."

"So, no contact?" Cate impatiently asked.

"Right."

"So, if there's no contact, how did Kyle find out? Ed, I know you. You wouldn't tell him."

"No contact with you and Robbie, and nothing can ever be disclosed about your relationship," Edward recited in a lowered voice as if reading from the document.

"I'm guessing his phoning me was a loophole," said Kyle.

"He called you?" Cate's anger seared. "Why?"

"He's out of money," Kyle casually inserted.

"How can you spend two hundred and fifty thousand dollars in six months?" Cate was aghast.

"Don't forget," Kyle noted, "he also had Robbie's eighty-thousand dollars in addition."

"So, Kyle, what did you say?" Cate examined Kyle's behavior.

"You sure you want to know?" Kyle set down his drink, preparing for her reaction.

"Yes, word for word." Her temper was ignited, her breathing penetrating.

Kyle and Edward stared at each other, curbing their amusement.

"Okay. When Alex demanded another two hundred and fifty thousand dollars, I said, quote: *go fuck yourself* and hung up."

As the men laughed, Cate's cheeks flushed.

"It's hard to believe my sister's an adult," Edward guffawed. "Her delicate ears can't handle foul language."

"She can repeat the lines in a script, though," Kyle cited, "In *Piercing Heat*, the swearing from her mouth in the movie, my goodness gracious."

"Yeah, I had to prepare our mom to be shocked by her little girl," Edward taunted.

"Will you two stop," she reprimanded. "Can we please stay on the subject? Do we need to worry?"

"No, I served him notice he was violating the NDA, and no contact meant the entire family, including Kyle. Should put some respect in him for the rule of law."

"Good." She removed her phone, "Ed, I'm calling our accountant to transfer that amount to you at once. You may not let us give you the money for Robbie's trust, but we're giving you this."

Edward seized her phone from her. "I've already told Kyle no."

"Let's not argue." Kyle pushed aside his empty glass, "I have this worked out. I'll deposit two hundred and fifty thousand dollars in Emily's trust account. Medical school's not cheap. You can't refuse our gift to Emily."

"Okay, I give," smiled Edward. "As long as it's for Emily."

"Come on. It's our last night together," said Kyle as Cate stole a taste of Edward's drink. "Let's make an early toast to the new year."

Edward poured everyone fresh drinks.

"Well, I'd say 2015 started off all right." Edward noted Cate's Oscar on the mantel. "It went downhill from there. Mom died, we almost lost Kyle … 2016 has to be better."

"Yeah, a new adventure," Kyle agreed.

Cate was silent, her stare vacant.

"Catherine?" Edward's concern brought Kyle's attention to Cate's distant air.

"Honey?" Kyle rose to go to her, bringing her back to reality. She put her hand up and motioned to stop him. Kyle lowered himself down.

"We shouldn't be so hasty to forget everything we survived," said Cate. "It may have been a wretched period, but it showed the best of us. I learned how strong we are … kind, generous, brave."

Both men nodded.

"And Kyle, when I thought I might lose you, life seemed hopeless. I was so alone." Cate took his hand. "And then I discovered I wasn't, never had been. I have Ed and our children." She raised her glass to them. "So, I pay homage to this past year because I'm surrounded by love. We all are. And that's what brought us through our darkest nights."

"To this day and the days to come," Edward toasted.

"I'm touched," Kyle added. "Only an indomitable spirit can find light where there was none."

As Cate blushed, Edward lifted his glass once more with a chuckle, "Someone tell a joke already before we all burst into tears."

Chapter 37
Heroes and Other Illusions

omorrow was New Year's Day, and Hollywood was busy making headlines. Everett Franklin had resigned his executive position at the studios in the wake of the controversy and impending criminal charges.

Late in the evening, after Robbie and Mia were asleep, Kyle read the news story aloud to Cate in front of the library's crackling fire, graphically detailing the case. The light of the flames shimmered off the Oscars on the mantel. Cate, spellbound, listened to the tale of debauchery and ruthlessness.

"Honey, I'm sorry you had to go through this crap."

Cate shifted clumsily on the loveseat and grimaced. "What happened to me was pretty mild compared to what some experienced."

"Well, you have guts."

"Yeah." She looked away nervously.

"The kids should know how audacious you are," he smiled.

Cate pulled her legs up under herself, a positioning reminiscent of a child, relatively small and tightly confined. "Kyle, um, there's something I probably should ..." She rifled her brain to articulate her fears. "I never fully explained why I left L.A. the first time."

Kyle was reading another trade's take on the news and was not aware of how strained her intonation sounded. "Yeah, the bullshit, right?" he replied coolly.

"Partly." She strived to get his attention, vehemently wishing she could slink away and hide. "Kyle?" It was vital for him to see her.

When he glanced at her, he observed how frightened she appeared. "Cate, what is it?" He moved beside her on the love seat. She wished he hadn't.

Tears pooled as she attempted to shake off the trepidation. She pushed herself further away from Kyle, compressing herself in the corner of the loveseat.

"I came to L.A. probably way too young to live on my own and start an acting career. I was so naïve and gullible." Her heart was pounding rapidly.

"I worked really hard. I went out on a lot of auditions right off the bat. Everything was falling into place for me." Cate turned away. "Until one day ..."

Cate lagged, staring at the floor, choking down a labored gasp. "Something bad happened."

She looked up at Kyle, his eyes lovingly set on her. "What, honey?"

Cate felt she might vomit, holding back the resounding emotions inside. "Maybe I should explain how it started."

She stared at the fire as if the words were written on the flames. "My dance instructor, Lisa, was older, and we'd sometimes get together after class to have coffee and give each other advice. I considered her a friend."

Cate cleared her throat. "One day, she invited a producer to our class. He never spoke to any of us, just watched. After class, Lisa called me and said the producer wanted to talk to the two of us right away about a project. She insisted I go and drove both of us to the audition." Cate inhaled, writhing to get to the point. "I trusted Lisa."

"When we arrived, nobody else was there. Of course, at the time, I didn't know ... I figured it out later ... it was all a scam. He wasn't a producer. He was a fraud." Cate closed her eyes and jerked her head. "My gut immediately told me to get out. I turned around to ask Lisa to drive me home. She was gone, leaving me there alone with him." The betrayal shaded her manner. "She set me up."

"I tried to run. I got to the door, but he grabbed me. He was faster and so much stronger. I fought, and he beat me down." Cate slumped in her seat, the back of her hand covering her mouth, muffling her speech. "I have no idea how long ... I was detached from it all, like an out-of-body experience. I heard this voice...this little girl crying and begging him to stop, and I realized it was me." She lowered her head, her chin touching her chest. "He threatened me when he was done and threw me out ..." Cate struggled to keep the tears from falling.

"I somehow managed to get myself to the free clinic. They wanted me to go to a rape crisis center to report it. I was in such bad shape, covered in cuts and bruises. It was tough to breathe because I had a cracked rib." Cate unconsciously rubbed the right side of her lower chest, exhaling the past. "No, I was terrified. I couldn't tell anyone. Not the police, not my mother. I didn't want anyone to know. I just wanted to wake up from the nightmare." Miserably, Cate glimpsed up at Kyle, scared of what she'd see. His vision fixed on her, an expression of horror and compassion.

"Oh, Cate." He reached out to console her, "Honey, I'm so ..."

She instinctively pulled away.

"I was so ashamed. Who else was harmed because I wasn't brave enough to go to the authorities?"

"You were young," Kyle confirmed.

As if lost in the haunting, lament swept her lips. "Nineteen."

The knowledge appalled him. Alarm masked his face, "Cate ..."

She dreaded the look she saw in his eyes, praying he wouldn't ask. But she knew he would.

"Cate, you were a vir ...?"

Cate's hand flew up to cover his mouth, blocking the syllable from being formed.

She peered at Kyle, tears welling, her chin quivering, defeated, and guileless. Grimly nodding, her hand slipped from his lips.

"Oh, God." Kyle rubbed his forehead, emotions invading his senses. The pain he felt for her was intense, but it was learning she had been so innocent that made him feel helpless, like witnessing the slaying of an angel. He searched for words of wisdom and solace, but his thoughts were jumbled, overwhelmed by mounting rage and despair. "Cate, you were so young and vulnerable ..."

Kyle paused. A more profound realization abruptly struck his mind. This is why Cate was deeply genuine, sweet, and often childlike. A part of her had never grown up; it simply survived. He had no words, only heartache for the woman he loved.

"I wasn't letting him win," Cate carried on. "I wouldn't be destroyed. I refused to go home. Instead, I spent the next four years working my ass off. Going out on auditions, being cast in small roles here and there, and doing well overall. At least I was supporting myself … and hating every minute. I'd go to an audition or do a shoot, and then I'd return to my apartment, curtains drawn, and sit all by myself with only the TV for company. I went nowhere, had no friends, no social life. Isolated. I was petrified of Hollywood, the people, the industry. In a way, he succeeded."

She paused, touched by the empathy in Kyle's eyes.

"Along came Alex. He was kind. At least then he was. And Alex rescued me from the loneliness. No big love story. An escape from L.A."

Cate gestured to the article Kyle had been reading, "So this was penance. I was doing what I should have done twenty-five years ago. I'm sticking up for the young girl I once was and ensuring no other woman will be hurt again."

"Did you ever tell anybody this?"

"Eventually, I told Ed. But not until after the four of us returned from the trip to Aruba in the spring of 2007. I knew Ed would accept me. He's a good brother. Anyway, Ed's the one who persuaded me to tell you. I've been scared."

"Why, honey?" Kyle slid forward to center on her hesitation.

"A few months after I told Ed, I brought it up to one other person, Alex. He was livid, saying he'd never have married me if he had known. In his opinion, it was my stupid fault for being in the situation in the first place … like I asked for it. He said I was 'nothing but damaged goods, a whore.' And he called me those horrible things again in front of our sons at the beach house." Shattered, she lowered her gaze.

Kyle fumed, attempting to suppress his anger. "Alex is a lunatic," he growled, gritting his teeth. "None of that crap is true, sweetheart."

Kyle felt a sharp stabbing in his gut. "You were afraid I'd react like Alex?"

"No, of course not," she defended. "I didn't want you to see me differently."

"Why would I?"

"Because, when I think about it, *I* see myself differently. *I'm* that broken girl, powerless."

Kyle reached out for her hand. Tentatively, she accepted his comfort.

"Cate, I know who you are. Nothing will ever change my love for you."

They were quiet for a while as Cate brought her sorrow under control, Kyle thinking how she had bared the broken pieces within her and that he needed to share his broken self with her.

There was one more secret to reveal.

"After … at the free clinic," she sighed, "the doctor told me that *sometimes, you just have to walk away.*"

Kyle's eyes grew wide with understanding, "Oh, Cate, the line from *Piercing Heat*. The violent scenes. It must have been traumatizing for you. I'd never have given you the script if I'd known."

"Yes, it was complicated. It was also immensely cathartic to use the pain productively." She pointed at her Oscar, "I wouldn't have one of those. Who ultimately won? I did."

Kyle scooped her into his arms. "Oh Cate, I'm so proud … No, proud doesn't begin to describe what I'm feeling. Cate, so much more. You're my hero."

"Kyle," she squirmed.

"No, you are."

"Honey, if anyone's a hero, it's you." Cate shifted awkwardly. "You took a bullet for me. How can you compare?"

"You're right. There's no comparison. What I did was out of love, an easy decision to shield and protect you. What you did was look evil in the eye and conquer it. And you did it alone. It takes real courage and resilience. It didn't destroy you. It doesn't define you." Kyle stroked her cheek softly. "Cate, you're amazing."

"Not damaged goods?" She peeked up, fragile helplessness about her.

"No, a gift from God."

The clock struck midnight. A new year was born. As they embraced tightly, capturing a sense of oneness, Kyle realized his biggest fear was losing her. Perhaps, he silently concluded, it was at this moment he had truly found her.

Chapter 38
Road Less Traveled

*I*t had been a transitional eighteen months for the family. To Cate's mind, life was speeding forward at an alarming rate. She craved time with her children. In his second year at Notre Dame, Scott left a significant hole in the family fabric. Robbie, eager to start college in the fall at San Diego State University, was a typical teenager preferring to hang out with friends than Mom and Dad. Mia, of course, relished being with her parents, particularly her frequent visits to their film sets.

Tom was behind his new desk in his redecorated office, shuffling a pile of papers. "So, how was your niece Emily's wedding in San Francisco? Two young doctors in love?"

"Fantastic," Cate said spiritedly. "Emily and Andrew were deliriously happy. It was lovely. And the boys were groomsmen, and Mia was the flower girl. Emily was the most beautiful bride."

Tom grinned. "Was Ed an emotional wreck?"

"He was a weepy Italian father," Kyle chuckled.

"I'm sure you'll be worse when Mia gets married." Cate nudged Kyle bouncily.

"I don't even want to think about it," Kyle lamented.

"Speaking of Mia," Tom said enthusiastically. "I received a call from the talent department at Disney. They saw Mia in your film, Cate. They were extremely impressed. Wanted to talk to you about Mia working with them."

"I don't think so," Kyle griped. "Mia's not even eight years old yet. Making a comedy with her mom is one thing. She needs a normal childhood."

"Mia's the daughter of two major film stars. It's part of her genes. They're talking about talent development ... acting, dancing, and singing classes. An occasional appearance on a preteen show. It could be an easy transition into a career for her someday. Consider it a fun after-school activity. Like soccer or piano lessons."

Kyle turned to face his wife. "Cate, I know you did commercials at her age, but your parents were with you. We can't be with Mia all the time. We work too much."

Cate took Kyle's hand, comforting him. "Tom, it's a wonderful compliment. But we need to discuss it and get back to you."

"No problem. It's a standing offer. No time limit."

"Thanks, Tom," Kyle said.

"On a different subject," Tom began. "Kyle, your directorial skills are earning you a stellar reputation. Especially having been up for a Directors Guild Award for the limited series last year."

"I didn't win," Kyle mentioned.

"Doesn't matter. You're highly regarded. You've caught the eye of a couple of the execs at Universal. Are you interested in expanding to features?"

Cate's smile broadened; Kyle looked skeptical.

"Flattering. I enjoy directing. I do. But I'm an actor. I'm at home in front of the camera." He slumped down on the couch.

"I understand." Tom set aside his notes from Universal.

"Wait," Cate argued, "why can't you do both? It might be complicated to direct while acting. Honey, you can do it. You have with me, especially in *Piercing Heat*. Consider it."

Cate viewed the tower of scripts in the corner of Tom's office. "Any worthwhile projects, Tom?"

He handed her a script. "Great part for you, Cate. Have you ever wanted to be a *Bond* girl?"

"No," Cate made a disapproving face. "I wanted to be the super-spy."

"Okay. Well, here you go. This fits your wish ... especially if you'd like to work with four men."

"Oh, are they the *Bond* girls, then?" Cate kidded.

"No," Tom laughed, "they'll be your four cohorts."

"Intriguing." She turned the pages, looking for the principal male character's description, "What's the male lead like?"

"Like Kyle Weston. It's an action thriller with humor and a nice kick to it. It starts shooting in a couple of months. And no nudity, Cate."

"You have me sold." She passed the script to Kyle. "I'll do it if you do it."

Kyle paged through the material, "Don't you want to read it?"

"I trust Tom. He hasn't steered us wrong."

"I'll read it over first, Tom," Kyle smiled, taking Cate's hand and moving to the door. "And then Cate will talk me into it."

Leaving Tom's office, they strolled to their new 2018 cardinal red Mercedes Roadster convertible. Cate's forty-seventh birthday present from Kyle.

Cate squeezed Kyle's hand. "Could this car be any more 007?"

Walking toward the driver's seat, Cate snatched the keys from Kyle. "My present, I'll drive, thank you. You can read over the marvelous script and describe it to me on the way."

Revving the engine, Cate turned on Sirius radio.

"So, when do you want to discuss Mia's offer?" Kyle asked, opening the script.

"When Mia gets home on Sunday. Don't you think she should have just a little input?" Kyle took an exasperated breath. Cate admitted her husband's fatherly reservations.

Turning another page of the script, Kyle sulked, "Cate, this is more than a little challenging."

"If anyone can do it, you can," she assured as Foreigner's *I Want to Know What Love Is* came on the radio.

"Here we go," Cate joked. "What's your best memory?"

"Cate, after all these years," he jibed, "what do you think?"

"The back seat," she giggled. "You were such a naughty boy."

"And your best memory?"

She was silent, and then a huge grin appeared. "Right now, sitting next to you."

Kyle smiled and rechecked the script. "This'll be fun."

"Fun's good. We could stand some fun in our careers." She gunned the car and sped down the highway.

Nearing the beach house, Kyle momentarily turned down the radio.

"So, beautiful wife, we have an empty house this weekend. Let's drive up the coast."

Cate's eyes sparkled, her hair blowing in the breeze as they drove north on Highway 1, the Pacific Ocean at their side.

"I say we stop around Santa Barbara," he proposed. "We'll spend the night."

"Kyle, we don't have any clothes with us."

"Never stopped us before. Did you forget Labor Day weekend years ago when we first saw our land in Montana?"

As *Iris* by the Goo Goo Dolls serenaded them, scenting the air with romance, Kyle opened the script again to find the name of Cate's character. "Tear up the road, Tasia Luca."

Kyle began singing along with the Goo Goo Dolls, coaxing her to join in.

Chapter 39
Way Down

A modern-day thriller, *Way Down* was a sharp script with clever twists. Cate's role allowed her to wear distinctly provocative costumes, disguises and perform different "characters" in the intrigue's commission. She was also charged with the lion's share of the action-packed stunt work. It made for a unique change-up.

During the shoot, Cate and Kyle rented a two-bedroom penthouse suite in the Manhattan hotel on the New York location. When Mia was not in town with her parents, her bedroom became Kyle's office space to plan the next day's shots. Kyle was meticulous in translating the script to visual dynamics, often working late into the night. Kyle was genuinely fulfilled with this project, directing and acting. And Cate knew he was good at it.

Mia came to visit her parents on location a few times. Enthralled by the filming, she would sneak to the stage. However, it was not an appropriate shoot for Mia to stay the entire time. Unlike her brothers, it would be impossible to keep her in the trailer with a tutor. So, while her parents worked, she happily alternated between Uncle Ed's and Aunt Julia's houses.

Mia honestly couldn't wait for this final trip to New York to visit her parents and the *magical* production. What excited Mia was being on set and seeing the mechanics of running a movie project. Cate, protectively, verified today's scene was free from foul language.

After the first take, Mia shouted, "Mama!"

Cate turned to spot a blur of Mia running full speed to her.

"Sweetheart, how was it?" Mia threw her arms around her mom's waist.

"It was cool, Mama. You and Daddy are so good together. I wish I could act like you do."

"Honey, you're a wonderful actress. Very natural. Maybe I can talk Daddy into letting you do another small part in a comedy with me? What do you think?"

"Mama, please, will you?" Mia tightened her cling. "What about Disney?"

Cate held Mia at arms-length and examined her expression. "Daddy and I are still considering Disney's offer. Don't worry." Cate winked at her daughter with a wily glint. "You must have Daddy or me working with you until you're older, deal?"

"Okay, but I'm ready. Just look how tall I am!"

"I've noticed, Mia … and, in my opinion, you're growing up way too fast."

Kyle walked up and kissed Mia's cheek. "Hi, sweet girl, did you see?

"Yes, Daddy, it was great."

"Well, thank you, baby girl." He tickled Mia, and she giggled. "Mia, your parents need to do another take of this scene." He gestured to Cate, who nodded in agreement. "You can sit over there quietly and observe."

"Yes, Daddy. Love you, Mama." Cate kissed Mia and moved to the first position on the bedroom set.

The process transfixed Mia. She couldn't wait for her opportunity to stand in front of the camera.

Chapter 40
What You Deserve

*T*he scene was the climax of the action. It was a rough cut. Kyle let Cate critique it after multiple edits and angles. Kyle dubbed in some temporary background music to enhance the action sequence. Because of the tempo, he used Dark Horses' song, *Alone*, and at the end, Kaleo's *Way Down We Go*.

"And action."

Scene: The villain, Rothchild, and his henchmen have apprehended the crew. Rothchild's thugs guarded Bumper (ex-military), Walt (former British Intelligence), and Trip (an MIT computer genius), all handcuffed and disheveled from a bloody beating outside the open doorway. Cate's character, Tasia Luca, a legendary thief, was apparently missing, having quit the team a couple of days prior.

Kyle, playing the elite team's mastermind Brian O'Malley, also handcuffed, was hauled by the back of his jacket's collar to Rothchild's private office and thrown on the floor. Rothchild's personal guard was inside the office adjacent to the door. Rothschild cackled menacingly from his desk as he watched the arrangement of captives around his office.

Cate became engrossed in the story on the screen, welcoming Kyle's perceptive direction of the action. Kyle watched Cate intensely, studying every contemplation navigating her face while she viewed the rough edit.

On the screen was the beginning of the rescue.

"Augustus?" Tasia cooed, holding a .22 pistol.

As Rothchild turned, Tasia shot him between the eyes. Tasia had also blown away his guard before Rothchild's lifeless body could hit the ground.

Tasia vaulted toward the team. Flipping the gun into her left hand, she grabbed a dagger from the desk and expertly flung the blade into the chest of a thug who was aiming to shoot Walt. The impact caused the shot to miss, the thug falling backward, dead. With two more quick steps and a leap, she landed on the other guard, slamming him back to the ground.

Tasia stood on him with her stiletto across his throat, the .22 pointed at his skull. "In the mood to join your boss?" Tasia purred sensuously. The henchman dropped his gun as the guys cuffed him, knocking him unconscious.

Cate's face glowed with anticipation, glued to the skirmish on the screen. Kyle enjoyed Cate's delight, prizing her appreciation of what he had captured on film.

Tasia walked into Rothchild's office and stooped in front of O'Malley to unlock his restraints.

"I thought I said no guns." O'Malley held up her gun with a royal blue grip.

"It went with my outfit," Tasia teased.

"I never doubted you," O'Malley stated.

"I told you. I'm gifted at what I do. Unpredictable and proficient. But I'd never betray a friend."

"So, we're friends?" O'Malley set her gun on the desk and removed his leather jacket, holding it for Tasia to put on over her torn blue dress.

Tasia gratefully put it on. "I'd like to think we are … aren't we, Brian?"

"Yes," he said tenderly, adjusting the jacket's lapels on her. O'Malley picked up Tasia's gun, handing it back to her.

The lights came up in the screening room.

"So, first impression? It's rough."

Cate was bubbling with enthusiasm. "Kyle, it's fantastic. You made me look like a superhero. So full of action. Show me more. I love it."

"It's coming together well. A lot of editing to do."

She kicked up her feet to relax. "Kyle, it'll be a blockbuster."

"We may have to make a sequel."

"Wouldn't that be fun?!" Her smile tickled him.

He stared at her with a roguish grin, putting his hands behind his head. "This may be one of the best choices we've made career-wise."

"Better than two Oscar-winning performances?" She was flabbergasted.

"Yes. This set-up could be a franchise. And it was a hell of a lot of fun. A cast with great chemistry. And a superhero." He flirtatiously bumped Cate, which made her laugh. "And you were unbelievably sexy. I'm guessing you're getting over your shyness."

"Only because it was done with plenty of humor."

The disbelief in his narrowed eyes was easy for Cate to read.

"Okay, I trust my director," she confessed endearingly.

Kyle reached over to kiss her. They sat alone in the dimly lit screening room in the movie theater seats, savoring the moment.

Chapter 41
Accolades

The publicity run for *Way Down* was nonstop talk shows, interviews, and public appearances. It was the first occasion Cate and Kyle interviewed together for the same film. Usually, it was a *divide and conquer* philosophy for hyping a new release. It was essential to Kyle they do at least one major talk show together. Derrick Morton won the draw.

"*Way Down*, the highly anticipated action thriller, opens in theaters across the country this Friday. Here are the film's stars, Kyle Weston and Catherine Leigh."

Walking out, waving, they made their way to be seated next to the interview desk.

"What a treat to have you both on the show. Let me begin by asking a basic question since you're married. Is it difficult working with your spouse on a production?" He threw the question to Kyle.

"Not at all. Cate and I had acted together long before we were married. This is our fourth film."

"So, you're fond of working with your husband?"

"Yes, of course," said Cate, "I appreciate performing with talented actors. I'm a little biased, but I think Kyle's one of the best."

"Well, Kyle, you not only starred in *Way Down*, but you also directed. Challenging, isn't it?" Morton shuffled his cards to a new query.

"You do view the material from a unique perspective when directing. You need to see everyone's place in the structure and how they interrelate. Your focus is the overall picture instead of simply your contribution as an actor."

"So, Cate," Morton grinned, "set the stage for us."

"Sure. This scene takes place the night before our team, consisting of four men and me, set a risky plan in motion. I play Tasia, a thief, and Kyle is O'Malley, the crew's leader. Tasia's trying to find someplace to rest."

"Here's *Way Down*," Morton said as the clip started.

Tasia snuck into the bedroom, gingerly unzipped her jeans, and removed them. She was dressed in her underwear and a tight tee-shirt. She crept over to the bed where O'Malley slept and slowly pulled back the covers. It appeared she was being careful not to disturb O'Malley. Then Tasia plunked down hard on the bed, yanking the blanket over her and off him.

"What the hell ... hey!" O'Malley sat up.

"Walt snores like a freight train, and Bumper's fumigating the place with farts," Tasia stated. "I'm not staying out there with them."

"You wanted to be treated like one of the guys."

"Move over. I'm good at what I do. That's why you hired me."

"So, you thought you'd move in?" O'Malley pulled the covers back onto him.

"You expect me to be functional tomorrow, then I need some rest." Tasia made herself comfortable.

"Why don't you go bug Trip and sleep in the computer room with him?"

"He's kind of cute ... way too young."

"Wait," he squinted at her. "Weren't you trying to find a quiet spot to rest?"

"I'm attempting to remain professional," Tasia said coquettishly, then showed her real annoyance at his suggestion. "Yes, of course, a place to *sleep*."

O'Malley slid his arm behind Tasia and leaned forward toward her lips.

"Hey, don't get any ideas!" Tasia drew away.

O'Malley snatched his pillow from under her head and handed her another.

"Relax … *my* pillow. Here, you can have this one."

"Fine. Just keep that thing away from me." Tasia rolled over onto her side, facing away from O'Malley.

"How I've missed your winning personality." O'Malley rolled in the opposite direction to sleep.

The studio audience briskly applauded.

"Very, very funny," Morton commented.

"The script is well-written," said Kyle, "and full of humor."

"I heard about some interesting situations on the set," Morton chattered. "First, there's a scene where Cate performs the old Patti Smith song, *Because the Night*, in the movie. And then a workout competition between you, Cate, and costar Noah Byers, who plays Trip."

"Yeah, the song was inspired by a contest years ago in Aruba. Cate was quite invigorating."

Cate tried not to blush. "Kyle instructed me to be seductive and belt it out. And I do what my director tells me. I choreographed it myself."

Kyle's eyes grew large, hunting for the best words. "Cate made it erotic."

"Ooh, I'd like to see that," Morton chuckled.

"You'll have to go to the movie," Cate coyly bantered.

"And what about the workout?"

"You mean the nonstop sit-ups and planks?" Cate grimaced. "It was excruciating."

"The guys kept cracking up," Kyle added, "causing multiple takes. I think Noah cried *uncle* first."

"My muscles were screaming." Cate turned to Kyle. "You guys were mean."

"You have sexy abs," Kyle bragged.

"Well, we happen to have a picture of you and Noah after the workout," said Morton, showing a photo of Cate and Noah holding up their tee-shirts to show off their stomachs.

The audience laughed, applauded, and hooted. As Kyle joined the merriment, Cate dipped her head down to block the embarrassment.

"Hmm, nice," Morton observed.

"Noah's abs are better than mine," Cate jested.

A female audience member loudly yelped.

"See what I mean," Cate trained on the woman and giggled. "We did have fun making the film."

"I'm looking forward to seeing it. *Way Down* is opening this Friday in theaters everywhere. It's been great catching up with both of you, and good luck with the film. Everyone, Catherine Leigh and Kyle Weston."

As they exited the stage, waving to the crowd, Cate mumbled with a twinkle to Kyle. "I'm gonna get you for that one."

Putting his arm around her, Kyle smiled and whispered back. "Bring it on, gorgeous!"

Chapter 42
A New Direction

Being in the central time zone two hours later than the event made it difficult to stay up late when Scott had an early class in the morning. His girlfriend, Erin, had fallen asleep long ago on the couch. Still, Scott had to watch the Directors Guild Awards to see if his dad would win for *Way Down*. Scott sat on the floor, his back against the couch, viewing the live feed on his laptop, fighting to stay awake.

Finally, the award …

"And the Director goes to … Kyle Weston for *Way Down*."

Cate kissed Kyle, who made his way to the stage.

"I want to thank the Directors Guild for honoring me with this award and everyone involved in this production. I'd like to thank my family, especially my children." He stared at the large plaque. "I became a director due to a fateful night. I was happy being an actor until it was almost taken away. And I discovered I loved directing. This award confirms that life-changing events can have a positive outcome. A shot changed the course of my life, uncovering a path less traveled."

Kyle gazed at Cate in the audience. "Cate, you gave me the strength and belief in my abilities to fully realize who I am and what I have to contribute. Without you, I wouldn't be here. I love you. Thank you to everyone."

Scott's face lit up, "All right, Dad."

Erin stirred. "What happened?"

"He won!"

"Darn, I missed it. Sorry." She sat up slowly, peeking over Scott's shoulder.

"It was good. Dad and Mom were happy. Let's get to bed."

Chapter 43
Sunrise Over the Hollywood Hills

The tradition lived on. Standing on Edward's deck, Kyle topped off his glass and twisted the bottle into the champagne bucket full of ice. Edward shared the evening with Beverly, lying beside each other on a double lounge chair. Cate sat in a chair with her feet propped up on the railing, her evening gown draping onto the slate floor.

"Didn't I make a toast a while back that we'd be celebrating more awards?" Edward grinned. "Nailed it!"

"I never imagined it'd be a DGA," Kyle shook his head. "I'm still overwhelmed."

Cate pursued, gleaming with pride. "I knew you had the talent and determination, dear husband. And you've always been rather bossy."

Everyone laughed again.

"So, what's next?" Beverly asked, sipping her glass of champagne.

"A break." Kyle slid a chair over to Cate's and copied her posture.

"Oh, come on," Edward complained. "You two can't sit still for long. What's in the works?"

"The studio's clamoring for a sequel to *Way Down*," Kyle admitted. "It has to be right. It needs to be well-written like the original."

"No, better," Cate confirmed.

"First, we're taking time to celebrate our tenth anniversary, which we had to postpone." Kyle glanced at Cate amorously. "Just the two of us."

"So where to? You've been nearly everywhere overseas." Edward tasted his glass of liquid bubbles.

"It might be nice to go to the ranch," said Cate, turning her body toward Kyle.

"Definitely." He kissed her.

"Well, Uncle Ed would be happy to watch Miss Mia."

"Oh yes, Mia's so sweet," Beverly agreed.

"You might have to fight Julia for the honor," Kyle warned.

"Hey, she's *my* niece. I get first dibs!"

"Do you mind keeping Oakley again too?" Cate asked. "They're a set, you know. Wherever Mia goes, Oakley follows."

"Love that dog," said Edward.

"May I make a toast?" Beverly invited. "Happy anniversary to the most wonderful couple. Ten years is astonishing in Hollywood."

Kyle clanged his glass with Cate. "It was four years before that when I experienced the best evening of my life."

"So true," Edward joked. "That's the night you met me."

More laughter …

"Yes, in a way," Kyle granted. "I owe you, Ed. If you hadn't dragged Cate to the party, I never would've met her."

"And if you hadn't abandoned me dear brother, I never would've accepted a ride back to your house with Kyle."

"So, my philandering days were beneficial, after all," Edward laughed.

"I still loved my big brother, even then." Cate blew Edward a kiss.

"I didn't see you all week, did I?" Edward finished his glass and dug in the wine cooler for another bottle.

"No, not really. I spent the entire trip with Kyle." Cate smiled at the memory.

"It was the beginning of a beautiful friendship." Kyle rubbed the back of his hand against Cate's flushed cheek.

"Gosh, this is romantic," Beverly gushed.

"You have no clue how hard we fought for it not to be romantic," Kyle observed. "To be strictly platonic." Kyle took Cate's hand, kissing it.

"Except Mr. Buttinsky here," Cate jibed, glaring at Edward. "He kept trying to get us to admit we were in love. Messing up the friendship."

"Of course," said Edward. "I never saw two people more in denial of their true feelings."

"It worked out." Cate hugged Kyle's arm.

"Yes, it did," Kyle reciprocated, turning the spotlight on Edward and Beverly. "So, what about you two?"

Beverly stared ravenously at Edward for a positive response. Cate was amused by Beverly's intensity and Edward's expected uneasiness, deciding to rescue her brother.

"Kyle, don't pry. Relationships are complicated ... as we know," she said with a wise look.

The sun had almost wholly risen in the morning sky. Edward and Beverly seemed content. Cate and Kyle viewed the brilliance of the Hollywood skyline.

Kyle leaned toward Cate and softly spoke, "Right here on this deck nearly fourteen years ago was the beginning."

Cate nested against her husband's shoulder. "How far we've come ... how much closer we are."

Kyle gently kissed her cheek. "So, for our anniversary, we're going home? The two of us."

"Sounds heavenly." She closed her eyes, cherishing the idea.

Chapter 44
Our Story

Cate sat in the meadow, keeping company with the grazing horses. Her laptop was open, and she was busy typing. Mia was spending the week with Uncle Ed and Beverly, where she'd experience perpetual shopping trips. Cate and Kyle's belated tenth anniversary was set for privacy and romance in their ideal home.

Kyle approached the gate with carrots, the horses galloping toward him.

"You're spoiling them," Cate noticed.

"Trying to bribe them into liking me as much as you."

"Animals love me. It's part of my DNA." She continued to type.

"I have an idea," said Kyle, feeding his horse, Ramsey, a snack. "What if we go to town and catch a movie? We haven't been alone at the movies in ages."

"How fun! Give me another half hour, and I'll be at a stopping point." Her fingers clicked fiercely.

"Stopping point? Whatcha workin' on there, sweetheart?"

"I decided to write a book." She bit her lip, concentrating on the story.

"Oh." Kyle craned his neck, although he was too far away to make out anything. "A new career? Giving up acting?"

"No, never," she puckered her brow. "But I'm thinking of cutting back. I want to have more time with Mia. Maybe take her to classes at Disney. And spend time with the boys when they come around. I miss my kids."

"I could also cut back," he offered. "You're right. Mia's growing up fast, and, gosh, our boys are in college! I miss them, too."

Cate's eyes glistened, nodding an enthusiastic appreciation.

Returning to her laptop screen, she reread what she had written.

"Maybe I'll turn it into a screenplay," she hinted.

"What's it about?"

"It's a story of two friends."

"Friends?" He grinned while Cate's horse, Blossom, nuzzled him for more nibbles.

"Uh-huh," she mumbled, her mind locked on the manuscript.

"Like a buddy film?" Kyle fed Blossom another carrot, patting the horse's nose gently.

"Kind of, except it's a man and a woman."

"Interesting, tell me more." Kyle rubbed his hands on his jeans to wipe off the dust.

"Okay, they experience a lot of life-altering situations together … always there for each other." Cate stopped typing.

"Really good pals?"

"The best." She extended her hand, beckoning him to come closer.

"Just friends?"

"Just friends," she shrugged bashfully.

"Well, there has to be an underlying or dynamic purpose to make the reader care about this relationship."

"What do you suggest?"

"Hmm. Well, he might be madly in love with her from the first moment they meet, but he keeps it to himself for an important reason. Perhaps, one of them is already committed to someone else." Kyle sat next to her, and Cate set the laptop on the grass.

"Fascinating. Of course, I believe in happy endings, so I may have to remove *that* barrier at some juncture."

"It makes sense." He brushed back her hair. "So, what's the happy ending?"

"I'm not quite there yet. A lot has to happen in between." Cate lightly tapped his nose. "Life is full of challenges and some sorrows."

"It's not living if there aren't struggles. Triumphs make the joy so much sweeter."

"Kyle, you're a poet."

"Nah, you taught me." He kissed her cheek. "So, tell me, does the woman love the man ... more than friends, I mean?"

"Desperately." She lovingly stared into his deep blue eyes.

"I look forward to reading it." He began to stand, but Cate reached for his hand, stopping him.

"Kyle, is it a silly, cliché story to write? A tale of love?" Her childlike uncertainty sought his reassurance.

Kyle caressed her face. "No, Catie, absolutely not. Our story is the most unique, special adventure of all." He kissed her with the fervor of the embrace in the darkened restaurant's banquet room in New Mexico years before. She slid her arms about him, reminiscent of the night, with no trepidation, no breaking away, merely the permanence of desire and yearning. Their rapture hailed that each touch was as if it were the first time.

Kyle took out his phone and played Harry Connick, Jr, singing *I Could Write a Book*. "A tribute to your manuscript."

Rising, he held out a hand to help her up. "May I have this dance, milady?"

"Always," Cate beamed.

"And forever," Kyle readily agreed.

Their love was full of music and joy, their passion never to subside. Instead, it grew with the years of intimacy. Cate and Kyle smoothly swayed, spinning and dipping, as they moved with zeal ... *and they laughed.* Kyle beheld this remarkable woman who won his heart fourteen years before, gazing at the garden lights dancing across a fountain's cascading water.

Tomorrow would be a better day for going to the movies.

The End

Biography
Antonia Gavrihel

orn to an entertainment family—her father a comedian and actor, her mother a big band singer—Antonia grew up accompanying her parents to soundstages, movie sets, and recording studios. Experiencing an exciting childhood, Antonia was placed in front of a camera at an early age. Although she loved acting, the dream of being a writer inspired her. Words, along with the visuals and stories they form, became her passion.

Back to One was created when she was raising her toddler, building a career, and managing the everyday hurdles of life. After settling her young son to sleep after work, she would write until the wee hours of the morning … for an entire year. Then began the twenty-five-year search for a publishing house to bring the novel to readers. In 2020, a serendipitous event would establish a flourishing association with Hidden Shelf Publishing House.

The first novel, *Back to One*, introduced the readers to relatable, engaging characters and was met with immediate success, rave reviews, and accolades. *Ambient Light*, the second in the series, reveals the deepening of Cate and Kyle's connection. Upcoming books in the series include *Cinéma Vérité*, exposing the darker side of celebrity, and *Slating Magic Hour*, entertaining a unique perspective of Cate and Kyle's friendship.

Aside from writing and occasionally acting, Antonia is a law professor and an enrolled agent/master tax advisor.

Cinéma Vérité (Back to One: Take 3) will be released by Hidden Shelf Publishing House in the Summer of 2023.

Follow Antonia Gavrihel at:
www.antoniagavrihel.com

On social media:
Instagram and Facebook
@antoniagavrihel

Back to One: Take 3
Cinéma Vérité

*T*he beach house was bursting with uninvited visitors—police, investigators, supportive friends, and loved ones. Everyone was intensely engaged in loud huddled discussions, no group paying attention to the other or respecting Cate's need to be left alone.

Near the front entrance stood the kids surrounded by their security team, headed by George but coordinated by Edward.

Cate crept unseen to the living room chair where George's coat was slung. Glancing around to make sure no one was looking, Cate reached inside the coat and carefully slid George's gun from its harness. The weight of the loaded weapon was surprisingly heavy, which made hiding the gun under her jacket awkward.

Taking a hesitant breath, Cate knew step one of her mission was accomplished. Now she could kill him. Step two was the tricky part … escaping the house unnoticed.

George caught sight of Cate heading to the kitchen and rushed to her. "Mrs. Weston. I thought you were going to try to rest."

"I was just straightening up, George. But could you do me a favor? I think I forgot my phone on the deck. Would you please get it for me while I hang my jacket in the bedroom closet?"

"Certainly." He turned and walked onto the deck.

As everyone remained preoccupied with their strategies, Cate quickly slipped out the kitchen door, which led to the garage and the outside world. She ran to her car, parked in the drive, and sped down the hill.

Step two … success.

Coming 2023

An Exclusive Bonus
Way Down – The Movie

The screenplay of *Way Down*, which Cate and Kyle shoot at the end of *Ambient Light*, was created for my curious readers. Many requests were received to share the story being filmed.

Scan the QR code below to receive the exclusive PDF or ebook of the entire movie script of *Way Down*, written in an easy-to-read style.